Beast Hunter

Beast Hunter

A Prequel Novella to *Kill the Beast*

Michele Israel Harper

Love2ReadLove2Write Publishing, LLC
Indianapolis, Indiana

Published by Love2ReadLove2Write Publishing, LLC

Indianapolis, Indiana

www.love2readlove2writepublishing.com

ISBN-13: 978-1-943788-26-2 (Ebook edition)

ISBN-13: 978-1-943788-25-5 (Paperback edition)

LCCN: 2017919606 (Paperback edition)

Library of Congress Cataloging-in-Publication Data is on file at the Library of Congress, Washington, DC.

This is a work of fiction. Names, characters, incidents, and dialogues are products of the author's imagination and are not to be construed as real. Any resemblance to actual events or persons, living or dead, is entirely coincidental.

Cover Design by Sara Helwe (www.sara-helwe.com)

ALSO BY MICHELE ISRAEL HARPER

Wisdom & Folly Sisters:
The Complete Story

The Candace Marshall Chronicles:
Ghostly Vendetta

Zombie Takeover

(Coming Soon)

Vampire Feud

Mummy Resurrection

The Beast Hunter Series:
Beast Hunter

Kill the Beast

Silence the Siren

(Coming Soon)

Quell the Nightingale

Slay the Wolf

Stop the Snow Queen

End the Fey

Coming Soon:

Altered Time Saga:
The Lady Bodyguard

The Lady Spy

The Lady Assassin

Standalones:

Queen of the Moon

Dreamworld

Stars Collide

The Ravens

Tales of the Cousin Kingdoms:

Ruby Dragon Kingdom

Diamond Unicorn Kingdom

Sapphire Griffin Kingdom

Emerald Pegasus Kingdom

Time of the Dragons

For my Grandma, Margaret Holmes.

You would have loved knowing that I now write stories instead of simply reading them. Thank you for all the books you shared with me.

1

Toes frozen, Rose sucked in a breath as the castle materialized before her and stretched far above her head. Moonlight blazed on the barren trees, lighting the forest as if it were midday.

It was time. The one night of the year she could see the castle—the castle no one else could.

Please, please! What are you doing in there? Can't you see what's going on? Can't you save us? her heart pleaded, but of course he couldn't hear her silent desperation, no matter how often she wished otherwise.

Rose sighed and dropped her gaze, her eyes darting around the too-silent woods. Cosette huddled nearby, complicit in this yearly excursion, even if she couldn't see what Rose could. Cosette gathered sticks and twigs—what was left of them—unhampered by the lateness of the hour thanks to the glaring moonlight.

Rose's eyes drifted uneasily over their surroundings.

Decay blackened everything and filled the landscape with its pungent odor. Rose struggled to remember what greenery looked like. It was the same night or day—black as far as the eye could see.

Cursed. Her land and everything in it. And there was nothing she could do about it.

Wait. No one was near them. Rose's breath caught. They were too far away from the huntsman. The huntsman they had dragged farther into the woods than he'd wanted to go, later than he'd wanted to be there, simply because Rose had to convince herself yet again that she wasn't imagining it. And he'd left them.

Rose growled low in her throat. Typical.

"Cosette! Come closer, love. I don't see…him." Whatever his name was this time.

Cosette nodded and picked up her basket, her weary sigh nearly silent, but like a gust of wind to Rose's ears. The quietest of noises revealed themselves to her like a crack of thunder at the oddest of times.

Rose looked for the huntsman once more, though she knew it was futile. What was his name? She never knew any of their names. Huntsmen streamed through her town, always on the prowl for the biggest catch. The highest reward from the steward. While she and her sister were forced to scrounge farther and farther away from the protection of the community. There was no food. No fuel. Commerce had all but ceased.

The huntsmen said it was the same all over the kingdom. Rose refused to believe it. The prince's people couldn't all be starving. They couldn't.

Her shoulders drooped. But they were. The prince's people were starving. The palace was inaccessible. Completely forgotten by all but her. And no one knew what to do. Least of all, her.

The villagers' eyes oft strayed to the silent castle, though not one of them could see it. If Rose questioned them, asking what they were looking at, they would blink as if coming out of a trance and laugh uneasily, clearly at a loss.

Not one of them believed Rose when she said it was still there. That it had ever been there.

She was swiftly taking Madame Savon's place as the town's lunatic.

Cosette settled her basket closer to Rose and began gathering twigs for their hearth once more. "We'll need to go soon, Rose."

"I know. Just a few more."

Rose moved to the next trap and checked it. Empty. Of course. She plodded to the next one, eyes drifting to the castle. A smile hovered about Rose's lips as her favorite daydream replayed itself.

The prince riding through her once-prosperous village. Before the silence. Before the riots. Before people withdrew into themselves, weary with hunger and hopelessness. Before the merchant ships sank. Before she'd lost her mère, and her père had lost his mind.

A young Rose had been cheering, waving a little flag with a blood-red rose on it, dancing in circles. She'd stumbled and fallen—right in front of the prince's horse.

She remembered the cries, the gasps around her while the rest of the crowd remained oblivious. The horse had reared. The prince had barely maintained his seat. And Rose had been certain she was about to die.

Père had snatched her away from the horse's hooves and cradled her close. He'd straightened and eyed the prince boldly when he'd brought his mount toward them.

The prince's ice-blue gaze had seared itself into Rose's memory. She couldn't look away then, and she couldn't look away now. Even though it was just a memory.

His entourage and guards had raised a fuss—to this day it reminded her of the hens clucking in their coop before the plague had taken them all. But the prince had raised his hand, silencing the chatter.

"Your name?"

She'd spoken at the same time as Père.

"Rosette."

"Her name is Rosette."

Warmth never entered the prince's eyes. His perfect face had been carved with a bland look Rose couldn't place. It both terrified and intrigued her. But he'd held out a single red rose to her.

"For the brave young lady, worthy of such a name."

Rose beamed. Père relaxed. The cheering near them resumed.

The prince had given her a bow from his seated position astride his horse and then had urged his mount on.

And Rose's heart had never been her own since.

Although her père had snatched her from under the horse's hooves that day, to her, the prince had saved her. He hadn't demanded punishment. He hadn't scolded her. Instead, he'd handed her his most prized possession. A beautiful, lush rose from his esteemed gardens.

A perfect rose for little Rose.

Even now the memory brought a smile to her blue lips. But memories were hard to hold on to when one's belly ached and vision blurred.

And no one had called her Rosette since Mère died. Her smile faded, and she forced her thoughts back to the prince and the silent castle.

Maybe the prince couldn't save them this time. It had been so long…

Rose's jaw tightened. *No!* He would save them. He would. She just had to wait a little longer.

Rose blinked. All the daydreams in the world wouldn't put food in her stomach or a fire in their stove. She sighed, checked to see if Cosette had followed her—she had—then bent to peer into the next trap. She paused halfway, arm still outstretched. She propped her hands at her waist, still bent, and tried to take a deep breath.

She couldn't.

Through her dress, she plucked at the stays that held her

captive. If only her sisters didn't insist on strapping her in so tight!

Fire lit in her. Her sisters. If only she had the strength to…no. The only one who mattered was Cosette. Only ever Cosette. The youngest, the one Mère had begged her to watch over before she slipped from this earth as silent as a shadow. If she kept Cosette safe, it didn't matter what the rest of their older sisters did. All five of the greedy little twits.

She tugged at the stays again, still shocked by how small her waist was now. Her sisters lounged and complained while she and Cosette worked their fingers to the bone and wasted away.

She thought about straightening, but it was too much work. She eyed the slender branch no longer propping open the trap's door. It was just out of reach. And it was beginning to get too dark to see it, thanks to a few clouds beginning to obliterate the glaring moonlight. Bless Cosette for following her on this night, when they should've been safe at home. Black spots swam in her vision. If only she had something to eat. If only she could breathe.

If only. Always, ever, *if only*.

Her eyes darted around the nearby forest. Cosette's bright-red cape—the only thing left to them that was made by their mère—shone through the barren trees, the moonlight hitting it just so. How had she gotten so far away again?

A low snarl did for Rose what she hadn't the strength to do for herself. She snapped upright and spun toward the growl, her world tilting dangerously.

A lone wolf, ribs straining against his patchy coat, swung his head between her and her sister. In a flash, every feature brightened, sharply illuminated, and Rose could see his entire being as if lit by a flame. His matted, filthy fur. Eyes ravenous with hunger, near insanity. Every muscle straining to hold perfectly still. One chipped tooth. Dull eyes, catching the moonlight every few seconds and throwing flashes of reflected light back at her.

Rose blinked, pulled the dull blade from her pocket, and shifted forward, crouched, ready to spring.

The rest of the woods dimmed further, but the wolf stayed brightly lit. The wolf and Cosette's red cape. What in all the realms?

The wolf eyed her, teeth bared, ribs heaving. Rose slid to the side, anticipating his every move, desperate to block the path to her sister. She instantly saw the path he would take and its outcome, and she staggered from its weight.

Cosette shredded, lying still in the crimson snow.

She blinked rapidly and tried to stay upright, only to find the wolf still crouched, ready to make his move.

Pick me, pick me, she silently pleaded. Desperate. Horrified. What had she just seen?

The wolf chose her sister.

She lunged. But she wasn't fast enough.

The wolf bounded through the patches of snow and black leaves, skirting Rose easily, on a path that led to the end of Rose's world.

She ran. She would never make it in time. She was too far away, and the wolf outpaced her with every footfall.

"Creator! Help me!" She flung herself after the creature. Cosette's head jerked up at her cry. Rose jumped up on a fallen log and launched herself at the wolf.

Impossibly, she landed before the wolf—between the wolf and Cosette. She had time for half a blink, then it toppled her. She plunged the dagger deep into its chest, the handle disappearing as they went down.

Her head cracked against something hard, and her scream cut off as the woods vanished.

"Rose. Rose! Please, wake up. Rose!"

Rose's eyes slowly opened. Cosette tugged at her, her strength pitiful. Rose couldn't move. Why couldn't she move? It was so warm… Her eyes drifted shut.

"Rose!"

Her eyes snapped open. Foul stench assaulted her at the same time she realized she still couldn't breathe. She hefted the wolf off her and tossed it to the side. The thing lay still and dim. No unnatural color about him at all. Rose cursed.

What in all the realms had just happened?

Cosette stared at her with wide eyes.

Rose jumped to her feet, then doubled over, struggling for breath. "Curse that blasted huntsman for leaving us to fend off the wolves ourselves!"

"It's better than what some of them try to do." Cosette's quiet words washed shame over her.

Rose gasped for another breath. Didn't she know it. But thanks to her brothers teaching her to grapple and to evade grasping hands, not one of the huntsmen had succeeded with either of them. And they never would. She wheezed.

"What is it? What can I do?" Cosette cried.

"My"—she gasped—"corset." Rose clawed at her chest. "Get. It. Off."

Cosette stared at her in horror for one moment before spinning her around and unlacing her apron, her dress, her overshift.

Rose tried to help, her attempts feeble. How had she just thrown a wolf like it weighed nothing, yet she couldn't help her sister with her own stays?

And how had she jumped in front of the wolf at such a distance, not brushing one of the trees that stood between them, for that matter? She couldn't wrap her mind around it.

Cosette's cracked fingers were deft, and she quickly had the threadbare garments over her sister's head and began unlacing her stays.

Rose gasped a full breath, then two more, just to remember what it felt like. "Don't...ever...wear a corset. Ever."

Cosette's mouth dropped open slightly—she was a lady through and through. At least, she would've been, had she been given the chance. Unlike her sisters. Snobs, the lot of them. Cosette's concerned look jolted Rose to the present. "Rose, surely you don't mean that!"

"Promise me."

Cosette often did what Rose asked without question. She searched Rose's face, then slowly nodded. The panic hadn't quite left Cosette's eyes. "Your color's returning."

Rose turned and stared at the wolf. The Creator had heard her. He'd saved her Cosette. Then why hadn't He saved Mère?

Her mouth hardened into a grim line.

She jerked away from the thought and attempted a smile for Cosette's sake. "What do you say we take this back to the village? The huntsmen will be glad to know, and we might even get some meat." She shivered, the cold blasting through her undershift.

Cosette's eyes widened. "Not until your clothes are back on!" She stuffed Rose back into her dress and hid the corset under a pile of black leaves. "Besides, we may not be able to get our teeth through whatever meat he has on him."

Cosette eyed the wolf doubtfully, but Rose could see the hunger in her eyes. The creature would be picked clean, what with seven sisters, two brothers, and a père who may or may not be present.

"Rose, how are we going to get him back to the village?"

Rose glanced at the pile of blackened leaves, then at Cosette's tiny waist, then the abandoned cloth peeking out from under the mound of leaves. A slow grin spread across her face. "I have an idea."

2

orchlight flickered as the huntsmen listened to her tale with apparent boredom, but the fire of greed lit their eyes. Scraggly though the beast was, it would still bring a handsome reward from the steward.

Rose was counting on it.

Rose shivered as a blast of freezing wind swept through their small town of Champagne, danced around the shabby houses, then howled off into the trees.

"You expect us to believe you killed a wolf singlehandedly. You."

The huntsman in charge eyed her. He clearly didn't believe her, nor did any of the others. Though the three men's eyes never strayed far from the carcass she and Cosette had hauled back on the makeshift litter made with their stays and aprons. Cosette would've died had anyone known the stiff material wrapped around the two poles, hiding beneath their large aprons, was their undergarments.

Rose bristled and stepped forward.

Cosette laid a gentle hand on her arm. "Monsieur, I assure you, every word my sister says is truth. She would not deceive you."

9

Rose relaxed. Her sister may have been the only person left in the world who believed in her, but oh, it felt like warmth and sunshine had returned to their world.

Madame Savon shuffled past, her stench and incessant muttering clearly identifying her in the moonlight that struggled against the clouds. "You should've let the wolf have her, girl. One less mouth to feed. One less person to watch starve."

Never! Rose lunged with a low growl in her throat. Cosette whimpered. Rose drew herself short from actually attacking the old woman, and glanced at her shaking hands. Was her self-control slipping so easily? Her hands twitched as she lowered them. But how dare the madwoman say such things about Cosette?

Madame Savon continued by without another glance in their direction, muttering about wolves, witches, and troublemakers. Rose wasn't certain which of the last two categories Madame Savon considered her. Maybe both.

Rose clamped down on the shout wanting to escape her mouth. Cosette would never be harmed. Not if she had any say about it.

One of the huntsmen started to speak, but a town crier called out at that moment. All turned to listen, hanging on to every bit of news possible. His horse's hooves pounded through the town as he repeated his message.

"The Mesdemoiselles of the Mountain are coming this way! Bring yer valuables. The Mesdemoiselles of the Mountain are on their way! Three months."

Rose's heart leapt. Food! The three women chilled her to her core, but they brought food. Somehow. Not a thing would grow in the entirety of France, yet they had food to barter and sell every couple of months.

Lights flicked on throughout the village, following the crier's path, then quickly extinguished as people saved their precious candles. Several came out of their homes.

The crier thundered out of the small village, off to the next.

Rose spun back to the huntsmen. Her eyes sought the one who'd started to speak, and her eyes demanded he continue.

"I can give you eighteen livres for the wolf's fur, and another five for the meat." He shrugged, looking apologetic. "Though there isn't much there, and it'll be tough as bark."

Rose stared at the huntsman, eyes wide. That much? She'd expected him to swindle her. The meat was worth half that. Less, perhaps.

After too long a moment of silence, the burly man broke it. "Fine, I will give you a hind quarter of the meat as well. But only after the steward has seen it. Deal?"

Rose nodded, her mind spinning with possibilities. If she made money from bringing in wolves… Could she do this? Be a huntress? Cosette would never be hungry again. Her family could eat. Her eyes trailed after the town crier. Maybe she could travel with the Mesdemoiselles' wagon…

He leaned forward. "But you will tell no one the huntsman wasn't with you. You will tell no one you killed the beast yourself. Understood?"

Rose's jaw clenched, but she nodded. She'd just have to kill another and take it to the steward herself. Her eyes drifted to the huntsman who'd deserted them, but he busied himself looking off into the darkened forest beyond the flickering light. She ensured he felt the heat of her glare, however. She turned back to the lead huntsman once the nameless huntsman started to squirm.

She held out her hand, her mind spinning with how much she was being paid for the wolf—how was that even possible?—and a weighted bag was placed there. She emptied the coins into her other hand and carefully counted each one.

Then she was running. She grabbed Cosette's trembling hand as she passed her and hauled Cosette toward their cottage.

Wait until her brothers saw this! Her père! Her sisters! They would survive.

Rose waited all that night. All the next morning. Past when the rooster would've crowed were he still alive, past when the sun peeked over the edge of the horizon, past when it blazed in the sky above, muted by thick, dreary clouds.

And still they all slept. Rose paced. How could her family sleep all day, then complain about the candles wasting away when they were up most of the night? They may have made and sold them, but they couldn't afford to waste even one candle. There was never enough, but their laziness made it worse.

A knock at the door sent her bolting toward it. She paused, then scrambled to hide the money pouch. Surely a thief would kill for the number of coins she'd received the night before. She turned and bolted toward the door once again.

Cosette calmly answered before she reached it, tossing a reprimanding look so much like Mère's, a pang shot through Rose's heart.

"Yes? Thank you. You are too kind."

Rose peeked over Cosette's shoulder. Her face fell. Oh. The huntsman they'd spoken with earlier. She'd hoped Père might come home. Then fear flared in her gut. Did he want the money back? Rose clenched her fists and prepared to fight. Well, he couldn't have it. Her family wouldn't survive without it.

He jerked his head toward the carcass dangling down his back, turning so they both could see it. "Where do you want it?"

Rose's mouth fell open. The entire wolf, gutted and stripped of his patchy coat, hung down the man's back, dripping blood.

Cosette opened the door wide and waved him toward their table. "So much meat, Monsieur? I thought we were to receive a portion?"

He stalked past her sister and slammed the bloody meat onto the wooden planks. The huntsman's eyes sought Rose's. "It seems tales of the Mademoiselle's bravery reached the steward before I did. He said to give you the meat with his blessing."

Rose snorted. He could keep his blessing. It was because of the steward their land was stripped of remaining resources so quickly. She wanted the prince back, not some upstart steward whose name she didn't even know.

She wanted her people to remember what they had lost.

The huntsman slipped an axe from his belt and deftly started hacking the animal into more manageable portions. It didn't take him long to finish. Must've been a gift from the steward as well.

Cosette spoke in low tones the moment he stopped, her gracious manner a rival to any Mademoiselle who used to grace the prince's court. "How lovely of him. Thank you for bringing it to us. There is freshly made mead in the kitchen, should you want any."

Rose shivered. Nasty stuff. She missed wine and fresh water and milk. The huntsman grunted, his axe now back at his waistband, and headed that way, his eyes darting around the inside of their home.

Rose wanted to object, defensive about the hovel, but Cosette lifted a warning hand. Rose grudgingly admitted to herself all of the cottages on this side of the village were the same, thanks to unimaginative and lazy builders. Rose started to whisper, but Cosette spoke over her, moving away.

"Thank you again. I will always remember your kindness."

Rose rolled her eyes. Kindness, her foot. The huntsman was only there seeking a smile from any one of Rose's lovely sisters. Too bad the entire horde was in bed.

She and Cosette were not nearly as lovely as the rest of the girls who didn't work. Rose's fists clenched.

She glared at the man who was supposed to offer protection, yet let two starving girls do his job. Mead trickled down his beard. He looked like a fool. She rather enjoyed it.

Cosette shook her head at Rose, then smiled at the departing huntsman before she shut the door softly. Rose stalked to her side and eyed the slab of wolf. If the shrunken thing could be called that.

"Do you need any help?" Rose asked her sister.

Cosette stifled her horror a moment too late. "Um, no, dear." Her smile turned impish. "I'd like there to be a little meat left when I'm done with it."

"I won't drop it this time. Promise."

Cosette shook her head. "I was more concerned it might go up in flames. It has to last as long as possible, you know."

Rose flushed. Cosette lifted on her toes to drop a quick kiss on her sister's cheek, then hefted the haunch of meat in her slender arms, leaving the rest behind.

Rose stood in the center of the room, tapping her toes. She glanced out the window for the hundredth time, trying to gauge the position of the sun through the clouds. "That's it."

Rose darted out of the room and tugged her two brothers from their shared bed. They were lucky there were only two of them, not seven. Their new cottage was far too crowded. Rose started to miss her old home—in the wealthy part of town—but jerked herself away. Such thoughts only caused agony.

"Claude! Pascal. Wake up! Come see."

Groans met her urging, but she prodded them the entire way to the table anyway, now cleared of the wolf.

Rose plunked the small bags of coins on the rough-hewn surface and waited. The sleep drained away as her brothers' eyes widened. She smiled. Exactly the reaction she was looking for.

She overturned the bag and let a few coins scatter across the part of the table not smeared with blood. She peeked behind her. Cosette was busily preparing the meat in the kitchen, out of earshot. She turned back to her brothers and leaned forward.

"I can trust you. Right?"

Nods and half-awake mumbling met her stern glare.

"This is for Cosette. Not Père. Not Bernadette, Yvette, Reinette, Nicolette, or Lynette. Just Cosette. She doesn't starve, and she never goes into the woods to hunt. Understood?"

"Aw, Ro, we don't even know when the wagon comes back through —"

She cut him off. "Three months. They will be here in three months. Buy as much as you can. You know the food never goes bad." Her eyes narrowed. "Somehow…"

Pascal slumped. "And to think I could still be sleeping. You buy it." He turned to go.

Rose latched on to his arm and hauled him back. She waited until her disgruntled brothers met her gaze. She eyed both of them, her gaze intense.

"I won't be coming back."

Pascal blinked. Claude's mouth fell open. "What?"

She nodded. "I'm going to go with the wagon. Find out if there's work hunting wolves. Or working the Mesdemoiselles' garden. Anything. I'll not stay here and watch our lives disintegrate into ash around us."

"Ro —"

"I don't want to —"

Her brothers' protests were cut short when she snatched the bag and starting shoving coins back into the leather pouch, her jaw clenched. She was done begging. She knew what she had to do.

They both jumped forward. "Okay, okay!"

"Fine!"

"Whatever you say."

She let the bag fall back on the table with a dull *clack*. Claude snatched it up, Pascal's fingers too slow. They scuffled over the bag, their eyes bright when they stopped fighting long enough to see its contents.

It may have only been livres, but it was more than any of them had had in a long time. So long. She turned to go.

"But how —"

"Where — ?"

"Why?"

She spun and pierced them with a glare. "It doesn't matter how I got it. Cosette eats. She wears shoes again. Warm clothes. And she works here, in the house, away from those dreadful huntsmen. I'll worry about where the money comes from. Do those things, and you'll have plenty." She hoped.

Pascal looked dubious, but Claude's eyes shone. It wouldn't take Claude long to convince Pascal of their good fortune. Anything to get out of work. A few more words should persuade them both.

"Do those things, and you'll have enough. More than enough. If I find Cosette is missing one of those things — just one! — you'll have to find a way to make the money yourselves."

Their eyes widened with every syllable of her tirade.

"But, Ro…"

The feeble objection faded into nothing.

Rose turned and strode from the room, each step singing of confidence.

Ro, she rather liked that name. Much better for a huntress than Rose. Yes, Ro. She could get used to that. She could —

Cosette peeked at her from the kitchen, a question in her eyes. Rose ducked her head and sprinted for their attic room. Three months. She had to keep the secret from Cosette for three months.

Or she'd never have the strength to leave her sister behind.

3

"Claude! Pascal! Come quickly!"

Ro's head lifted from the book she was devouring, and a frown puckered her forehead. Was that Père? Shouting?

"Oh, come, my daughters, come! Bernadette! Yvette, Reinette, Nicolette, Lynette! Come at once! Rosette—my darling little rose. Cosette! My pet. Make haste!"

Ro bolted the moment she heard her name. Père hadn't spoken it in so long. She collided with a tangle of sisters at the top of the stairs, the lot of them staring down the steps as though some madman had broken into their home and now threatened their very lives. Ro rolled her eyes.

Pascal and Claude pushed their way through the girls, and Ro followed in their wake.

The girls clomped down the stairs but refused to step off, once again clogging the pathway.

Père stood in the front door, letter in hand, beaming, his loose, now-gray hair blowing wildly in the blustering breeze. Ro's gaze jumped between the letter and the smile on his face.

He was smiling. Really, actually smiling.

She must be dreaming. She couldn't allow hope to blossom, not yet, but her traitorous heart beat wildly in her chest.

Her eyes sought Cosette's while her brothers demanded to know what the letter said. Cosette stood in the doorway, arms full of dried candles, blue eyes wide. The straggling sunlight shone through the window behind her, illuminating her gorgeous blonde hair for a glorious moment and making her look like the angel she was.

Cosette shrugged, a hopeful smile tugging on her lips, and they returned their attention to Père.

"Quiet now! Quiet now. It says"—he perched a pair of spectacles on his nose—"'Monsieur Michele Pierre Reynard the third, we make haste to inform you that your cargo vessel, the Jacqueline Rose—'"

Ro's heart squeezed at the mention of Mère's name. They may have lost everything, but the loss of that one ship was more painful than any other loss. Père had never been himself since that day. Well, not till today. She shook herself and paid attention.

"'—therefore we ask you to hurry to *le Port de Calais* and claim her fortunes. The ship is full to bursting, its cargo and crew intact.'"

Everyone cheered. Except Ro. A small smile blossomed on her face. Dare she hope? Her sisters flung themselves at their père, and her brothers linked arms and started singing and dancing around like the fools they were.

Père extracted himself from his children's hugs and blustered around, accomplishing nothing at all. "I must away at once. My horse. Where's my horse?"

"I've got it, Père." Claude dashed away.

"And I'll make sure your saddlebag is packed for a long journey." Pascal followed his brother.

Reinette squealed, her wheat-blonde curls bouncing, and called after her brother. "He doesn't need anything for a long journey, halfwit. He's coming back rich!"

"Ooh, ooh, ooh!" Bernadette pushed her way forward. "Bring a gown, Père. A ballgown. Dripping of lace, the best you can find."

As the oldest, Bernadette thought her word was law and the rest of them had to obey her merest whim. Ro snorted. She may have shared her eldest sister's dark hair, crystal-blue eyes, and willowy build, complements of their père, but that was where the similarities ended. She hoped. Bernadette was the worst snob of them all, and Ro dearly wanted to take her down a few pegs.

The rest of the girls shared variations of Mère's golden-blonde hair and lovely blue eyes, but Cosette was the only one who retained her gentle spirit. All the bickering? Well, Ro had no idea where that had come from.

"Bring me diamonds!"

"And ruby slippers."

Bernadette shot Reinette a scowl. "They don't make those, halfwit."

Reinette's deep-blue eyes flashed. "Chantrice had a pair at the last dance we attended in Paris, and I want ones just like them. No! Better. Diamond slippers! Teach her to stick her nose up at me."

"Bring me pearls, Père."

"Ah! I know. A peacock fan. Ten of them!"

The girls' voices joined as one, and they tried to outshout each other as they asked for the most ridiculous and expensive gifts they could think of. Things that had once been commonplace.

Père broke away, eyes on Ro. Her heart stuttered, and she drank in the sight of his smile, his lucid eyes, his attention on her.

"You have not yet said what you wanted, little Rose."

Her mind went blank, and she blurted out the first thing that came to it. "A rose," she squeaked.

Her sisters laughed, and Ro ducked her head.

"A rose? Simpleton. He could bring you a thousand roses!" Bernadette laughed, always the most outspoken and cruel of the sisters. Whether she meant to be or just didn't realize how she sounded, Ro wasn't sure.

Père gently lifted Ro's chin. As soon as their eyes connected, tears filled hers.

"A rose, dear child? Are you sure that's all you want? I could bring so much more."

She choked and nodded. All she really wanted to do was fling her arms around him and sob. How her heart ached at the sight of him!

Before she worked up the courage to slip her arms around Père, whom she feared might brush them aside in the next instance, or show her sisters the depth of her feelings, who would most definitely mock her for years to come, he moved on to Cosette.

Ro wrapped her arms around herself and turned away from her sisters, pretending to watch his exchange with Cosette. She really didn't want her sisters to see the tears spilling down her cheeks. Her entire being ached to feel his arms around her again.

"And what of you, dearest Cosette? What can I bring my little pet?"

Cosette wrapped her arms around his waist and stared up at him with adoring eyes, the loveliest blue of all. She didn't care what her sisters thought. Ro envied her. "Only you, safely back from your trip. There is nothing more I want in the world."

Ro shook her head. Only Cosette could forgive the last fifteen years in an instant.

The jeers and heckling started from her sisters almost instantly, but now they sounded much more poisonous.

"Well, of course she does. Pretty dresses wouldn't look fetching on her anyway."

"Thinks she's better than all of us, more like."

"Well, I think she's a snob."

Ro's eyes flashed. Her sister was the prettiest of them all. Well, she had been. And the kindest. She'd only taken two steps, rage boiling, when Cosette's hand wrapped around her arm. She looped her arm through Ro's and pulled her away, lowering her voice so only Ro could hear.

"Let's not give one of them a black eye today, dearest. Let Père's memory of his departure be a happy one."

"They shouldn't say such things about you."

"No, they shouldn't. But they do. You have to learn how to let it go, love. You can't control anyone but yourself."

"Yes, Mère."

Cosette's eyes glistened. "It's wonderful her ship was found, isn't it?"

All the fight vanished from Ro. Her heart ached with longing. "I'd give anything to have her back with us."

"Me too, dearest, me too."

"Well, I must be off!" Père beamed at them all, taking time to kiss each daughter's cheek and shake his sons' hands. Pascal held the horse still while Claude handed him his saddlebag. Their père thundered away, pausing at the gate to wave.

"Don't forget my dress!"

"Or my diamonds!"

"Who cares about you? Remember my pearls, Père!"

Cosette shook her head, and Ro directed a glare her sisters' way that was promptly ignored.

Père disappeared, and the siblings took their time to make their way back into the house, even with the frigid air that should've been warm and full of spring. Ro took a deep breath. Snow was on the wind.

Cosette clapped her hands. "All right, dear ones. Claude, Pascal, the barn still needs to be mucked and the animals fed. Girls, let's clean this house from top to bottom to prepare for Père's arrival."

Lynette yawned and sprawled across their threadbare

couch. "Why should we? He'll be months in returning, and by then we'll have servants to attend us. As it should be."

Her twin sister Nicolette joined her, shoving her sister's feet to the side and plopping down in the available space. "Yeah, who made you our boss all of a sudden anyway, Cosette?"

Both had honey-blonde hair and cornflower-blue eyes and had made quite a stir at balls in times past with their petite figures, demure smiles, and mischievous twinkles in their eyes. They could've been such fun, Ro was sure of it, had they not followed Bernadette in everything she said or did.

Cosette's eyes sparkled, and she gave them a good-natured wink. "Père did, of course. Just as he does each time he goes away."

Bernadette pushed into the room, displacing Reinette and Yvette, who were lounging against the doorframe. "I'm the eldest. I should be in charge."

Cosette offered her the basket full of freshly made candles she still held. "Then would you be a dear and finish storing the candles? I have no problem sweeping the room in your place."

Bernadette pulled away from the candles and wrinkled her nose. "And smell as you do? Never! Why we can't have beeswax instead of that awful-smelling tallow, I'll never know."

Ro crossed her arms, mimicking her brothers' poses. They grinned and said nothing, enjoying the hissing and bickering. Ro wasn't so laid back. Unfortunately. Each flung word filled her with more and more tension until she feared she would burst. Maybe a little teasing was in order, instead of the sharp retort she wished to fling her sister's way.

Ro smirked. "You mean since the bees all died? Or when the flowers stopped growing?"

Bernadette shot her a glare. "Thanks to you, Père's trip will take longer. He'll have to scour the entire countryside to find a rose."

Ro's heart dropped. Bernadette was right.

Reinette's face only held curiosity. "Why did you ask for a rose? Because of your name?"

She flushed. More like because of Mère's name. "I-I hadn't seen one in so long. I wasn't thinking—I'm sorry—"

"Oh, hush now." Cosette bustled around the room, cleaning things that were already clean but so threadbare, they might fall apart any second. "If Père truly has his fortunes restored, he can hire someone else to hunt for a rose for him."

Bernadette huffed and crossed her arms. "You know he won't. Anything for his precious Rose." She sent a glare Ro's way. As if Ro could be responsible for her own birth.

Pascal interrupted. "I can't believe you didn't ask to go with him, Bernadette, and acquaint yourself with your former beaus." Only Ro saw the teasing glint in his eyes.

Bernadette gasped. "Oh, no! Now why didn't I think of that?" She ran around the room graced with white-and-yellow décor, doing nothing of value, very much like Père had just done. "Quick! Help me get ready. Do you think I can catch him?"

Claude laughed. "Do you intend to walk the whole way?"

Bernadette stilled, her glare back in place, and huffed. "Whatever do you mean?"

Pascal shrugged. "We only have one horse, he is old, and Père needs to ride. By all means, run after him, but you'll have to walk the whole way to the Port of Calais."

"Oh, phooey!"

The boys looked at each other, then burst out laughing. Ro chuckled. She got the brunt of Bernadette's glare.

"Well I hope you are satisfied when Père searches the whole of France then dies when he can't find the one thing you asked for." Bernadette stomped out of the room and up the stairs, temper in full swing.

Ro raised an eyebrow as Cosette cried, "Now, that isn't kind! Come back and apologize this instant!"

Did Bernadette listen? Of course not. Ro wondered why Cosette even tried.

"Let her go, little pet. The room will be better for it." Claude winked at Cosette.

Lynette scrambled up from her sprawled position on the couch. "Wait! Dies? But what about my pearls?"

Cosette raised her hands, exasperation close at hand. Ro leaned forward, almost hoping her angelic sister would lose her composure. It would be a nice change from the even, level-headed saint who lived among them. Then again, she rather enjoyed having at least one sister who wasn't full of spite.

"Now listen, all of you. We do not know for certain that Père's fortunes are absolute. He may get there only to find the money gone."

Bernadette's stomping footsteps on the stairs halted. All chatter ceased. Each sister stared at Cosette with an expression of disbelief plastered on her face, including Ro.

The explosion of noise was almost painful.

"What do you mean?"

"How could you possibly say that?"

"First Bernadette wishes him dead, now you wish him—and us—destitute? What cruel sisters you are!" Yvette burst into tears. Her looks, somewhere between Cosette's and Reinette's with golden-blonde hair like Cosette's yet deep-blue eyes like Reinette's, belied a certain sweetness which was no longer present, thanks to constant bickering—her sisters' favorite pastime.

"Hush, everyone! Now wait a minute. Nicolette, Reinette—listen to me."

Ro let loose an ear-piercing whistle. Cosette cringed, but Pascal gave her a nod. "Nice."

Claude shook his head. "My sister. The greatest tomboy I know. I'm so proud."

Pascal chuckled. "At least she's the only normal one of the group."

Claude shrugged. "Except Cosette, of course."

Pascal snorted. "Anyone that calm can't be normal."

Both boys snickered. Yvette shot them a glare.

"That's quite enough out of you two," Cosette interrupted. She turned to the girls, raising her voice to ensure Bernadette heard, even though Ro was certain she was already hanging over the banister. "Of course we don't wish those things. We'd both be thrilled if he returned in perfect health and a little money besides. But the money is trivial. And not definite. We must prepare ourselves in case our fortunes do not come to pass, and we must work hard in order to survive until he does return."

Footsteps clomped back down the staircase, and Bernadette entered, shaking with fury. She shoved a finger in Cosette's face. "I, for one, am sick of living this way. I want my servants back. I want my own room. And I want it now."

Reinette let out a loud sigh. "Here we go again."

"I am not lifting a finger until Père returns with all of those things. Do you hear me? If you want to work your fingers to the bone, then *you* can be *my* servant."

She stomped out of the room, pounding up the stairs much louder than necessary, then slammed her door.

The sisters sat in silence, one brother staring at the ceiling, the other at the empty fireplace.

After a few seconds, Bernadette's door opened, then slammed again, rattling the windowpanes in the shabbily made home.

The siblings glanced at each other, then burst out laughing.

If there was more stomping after that, Ro couldn't hear it over the noise of their mirth.

4

Ro counted off the days until Père's return—and until the Mesdemoiselles of the Mountain arrived. Just in case.

Cosette confiscated the little pouch of livres from their brothers and hid it well until the day they could buy plenty of food, material for one new dress each—a working suit for the men, of course—and luxuries they had long been without, such as thread, needles, and wax.

If they even needed to do so after Père returned.

The other girls chatted endlessly of the mounds of things he would bring them, but Ro and Cosette never spoke a word of it, except to kneel in the little alcove used for prayers and implore for Père's safe return.

It was as if they spoke of it, their anticipated happiness might burst like a soap bubble.

Even Ro prayed. But if it shocked anyone, they never mentioned it.

And as she scrubbed dishes, made disgusting meals out of roots and scraps gained from the meager income of their candles, and mucked out stalls alongside her brothers, Ro's mind drifted often to her yearly trek, and how this year had been different than any other. How she'd left before the castle vanished with the rising of the sun.

How the wolf had blazed to life in the middle of the night, and how she'd been able to defeat him when it wasn't possible. But she never spoke of it, not to anyone.

And she tried numerous times to make something light up in the dark, all of its own. It never happened, and she never saw events play out in her mind before they came to be.

Must've been a one-time thing to save Cosette from the wolf, she thought, though it didn't keep her from trying to make it happen. Often.

Magic smiled as the man blinked several times, trying to take in the splendid sight before him. He stepped from the frozen, snow-laden ground onto the warm, spring path, crossing from the forest into the palace grounds.

Exactly where Magic wanted him. She waited until he was inside to close the palace gates. Of course, the old man took his time, staring at each orange tree, reaching out to touch leaves, then snatching his hand back as if he could erase the mirage with one touch of his finger.

Magic didn't care what he did once he got inside—the servants would be more than willing to take over. Simpletons. He could be there to murder them all, and they would still care for him as if he were the prince himself. It was sickening.

Magic told herself she didn't care what happened once he got inside the castle, but she couldn't help following him at a distance anyway. And even though each act of kindness from the servants disgusted her, she dared not interfere. His time here had to be perfect.

He enjoyed a splendid meal. A nap. Exploring the castle, each facet revealed to him as it had been in its days of glory. Another meal. Another nap. More exploring.

Magic wanted to beat her head against the wall. Maybe set something on fire, watch him scream and run. But she controlled herself.

Night came, the man slept, and morning rose over the castle wall, calling him to wake. And Magic sat in her stronghold and watched, head propped on her hand, bored out of her mind.

This could not be over fast enough.

After breaking his fast, the old man once more explored the castle. Magic tracked him at a distance, trapped in her room yet able to follow him in spirit, certain she would throw her plan to the wind if she had to watch every minute detail of his exploration. But wait. Something was different.

She sat forward. A gleam had entered his eye. He no longer touched things hesitantly, or explored as if he were on someone else's property; now he walked confidently through the rooms. He touched things with a sense of…ownership. He strutted about as a titled nobleman might, not a guest.

Magic sat back, a smile gracing her face for the first time since he'd entered the castle. Perfect. Her plan was about to be set into motion. Ah, how she loved greed in any form.

It was exactly what she needed.

He flew down the staircase, shrugged on his coat, and ran for the stables. Magic rushed to wake the beast. She only hoped she would be in time.

&

"Roses. Ah, yes. I need a rose for my Rosette."

Magic stood behind the man and his mount, pointing her staff to one of the roses. Though he couldn't see her, his eyes tracked down the long staff and halted on the flower.

"Ah, yes. Of course."

Magic smiled. Perfect. He grinned and plucked the flower from the vine, moving to tuck it in his jacket's lapel. Magic stepped aside as the beast let out the most frightful bellow. Magic laughed. Oh, the look on the poor man's face was priceless!

"How dare you touch my roses! And who gave you permission to pick one? I let you stay in my palace, gave you the best hospitality known to man, and this is how you repay me?"

Magic smiled. The beast was too deliciously cranky when he'd just woken up.

"For your insolence, you shall die!"

Magic rolled her eyes. Well now the beast was just being dramatic.

The man fell to his knees, crying and begging and pleading, telling the ridiculously boring story of his children, his misfortunes, and his daughter's request for a rose.

The beast froze at one portion of the story, just as Magic knew he would.

"I will forgive you your impertinence on one condition."

"Anything! Anything at all. Name it, and it is yours."

The beast grinned, revealing fangs and saliva and too many grotesque things to name. Magic shuddered.

"Your daughter. Bring her to me."

"I—uh—what?"

The beast scowled. "Give me your daughter in exchange for the rose, and you shall not die."

"I'm sorry. Wait. Which one?"

The beast snarled and threw out his hands. "Does it look like I care? Bring me the one who asked for the rose!"

"Oui."

The beast lost some of his ire and stammered. "Y-you agree? Just like that?"

"Oui. Quite right. Very well."

Even Magic's eyes widened. Would a père really care so little for his offspring? Her eyes narrowed. He must have something else in mind.

Nodding too many times, looking to be the complete fool

that he was, the man scrambled to his feet and backed away. "So…I am free to go?"

The beast marched forward, grabbed the man's collar, and lifted him into the air. Magic winced from the man's shrieks and gripped her staff tighter. This should be good. If only he quieted down.

"Know that you cannot escape your promise. Know that I will find you wherever you try to run—wherever you try to hide. Know that you are no match for me, mere mortal. And if you do not return with the girl, a curse shall befall you the likes of which you have never before seen." He threw the man. "Now go. And return with your daughter in two months' time."

Sobbing, the man scrambled away. He stilled. "Y-you mean, I-I-I have to come with her?"

"Go!" the beast bellowed.

The horse bolted down the long drive, and the man took off after it.

Magic approached the beast, who was staring after the man and his horse. "Well that was rather harsh, don't you think?" Of course the beast didn't answer her. "I wonder…can you even make good on your threat?"

She watched the beast carefully. The air surrounding him tasted of worry and hopelessness and despair. Exactly what she liked.

She smiled. "Didn't think so. I wonder. Will you ask me for help when the time comes?" Her smile grew. "And the better question: Will I give it?"

She studied him. No change. Shoulders slumping, he trudged away. Magic laughed. The girl would never come rescue him, no matter how hard he tried to find her from the confines of his magical cage.

How she loved to tease him with hope, then plunge him back into despair.

No girl would come, no girl would set him free, and no prince would ever emerge from the beast.

5

———————

*R*o sat in the alcove, her book nearly plastered to the scrubbed-clean window. Cosette had promised her as much time as she wanted to read in exchange for scrubbing all the windows.

Cosette knew exactly what it took to get something done in the least amount of time possible.

Ro huffed and dropped the book in her lap, rubbing her eyes. The muggy light was just so horrible! She couldn't use a candle, and she couldn't trust the sun to shine. She glared at the heavy clouds, a constant for far too many years. Curse whatever had brought this blight upon their fair land! She just wanted to see the sun shine again. To see something green and *alive*. To read without nearly going blind.

Her eyes dropped to the gate. It swung open, slowly, as if shifted by the wind. Ro grumbled and stood. And curse whoever had left the gate open, for the thousandth time, for vagabonds and pests to enter at whim!

A man in rags stumbled through. Oh, great. Just what she needed. To watch Cosette feed someone what they couldn't spare and then end up manhandling the beggar off the property herself.

She squinted as something odd scratched at her through her anger. He seemed…familiar.

"Our père, our père! He's home!"

Ro jumped at Claude's shout above her head. She spun around to see him fly out the door. She had no idea he was standing right behind her!

Siblings who'd made themselves scarce since his departure, hoping someone else would volunteer to do the many chores around the crumbling home, scrambled to the front door and crowded the doorway, trying to see what Père brought.

Ro backed away. Something was terribly wrong. Why did he look like that?

He wasn't riding. In fact, his horse wasn't with him. His coat, threadbare and tattered, was wrapped tightly around him, and he trudged forward as if he carried the weight of the world on his shoulders.

Cosette scurried out of the kitchen, face bright. Her eyes connected with Ro's, and her face dimmed. She immediately rushed to Ro's side and took her arm.

They stood like this, silent and waiting, both steeling themselves for what was to come.

Ro had always thought her sisters were stupid—well, except for Cosette, of course—but this was ridiculous. Not one of them noticed how Père looked. The state of his dress. His empty hands. True, it wasn't much different than before, but still. He should have blazed through the gate with finery such as they'd only dreamed of for so long.

"Where are they? Where are my pearls, Père?"

"Diamonds! Did you bring diamonds?"

"Are you vapid?" Bernadette pushed her way to the front. "Where is my ballgown, Père? I demand to be introduced to society. No wait. A new society. I want new friends, not those false people who abandoned us at the first hint of misfortune." She strained to see past him. "Where are the servants? Do they bear your luggage?"

Père pushed past them. Claude and Pascal stepped back from the mob of girls, staring at him with pale faces, tight jaws, and wide eyes.

Cosette and Ro stepped back as their père came toward them, steps dragging, the dead look back on his face. He paused, staring at nothing at all. Fear enveloped Ro's being. Oh, no. It couldn't be. He—he wasn't himself anymore. Again.

Her heart shriveled and turned cold.

Ro studied his face, hoping for a change. But no, nothing.

Cosette gripped her arm, fingernails digging painfully. Ro didn't care. Nothing mattered anymore.

He continued forward, then paused next to Cosette. His eyes stared past her, seeing nothing. "You have your wish, little pet. I am home. For all the good it will do you."

Cosette's eyes filled with tears, but she lifted her chin. "Nothing in the world matters more."

He didn't seem to hear her. He shuffled forward, then stopped next to Ro.

He shoved something into her hands, but she could barely look at it past staring at the blank look on his face. Something sharp pricked her finger, and dizziness consumed her, but she didn't care. She couldn't stop staring at his face.

"Your rose. You have no idea how much it cost me."

He stumbled into the sitting room, lowered himself into his chair, and stared into the fire. Just as he'd done nearly every day since Mère died and his ships were lost at sea.

Fury started to build. How dare he be so weak! How dare he not face what was happening—force his children to face it in his stead. Force *them* to care for *him*. He was no man. Not one she could respect, anyway.

She opened her mouth to tell him just that—she was done waiting and wishing and hoping for his return—when her sisters surrounded his chair.

"What happened?"

"You must tell us immediately!"

Pascal cleared his throat, a sheen in his eyes, "Oui, mon père, you must. What happened to you?"

That was the question burning in Ro's soul. What had happened to him? How did a person get to the point that he gave up and left, even though he was sitting right there? Ro's jaw clenched.

She didn't understand it. And she would never forgive him for it.

Cosette, always so in tune with Ro's every thought, squeezed her arm. "Patience, my love."

Ro growled. "I have been patient. Enough is enough."

Cosette shot her a concerned look the same time Pascal did. Claude moved closer to Père. "What of the gold? The treasure? What happened to our—your ship?"

Silence seized the room in its choking grip. The weight of the next few moments crushed Ro, driving the breath from her. Père's voice was so weak, so distant, she struggled to make her mind believe it was actually him speaking.

"Lost. All of it. Gone."

Questions exploded in a flurry around him.

"Quiet!" Pascal nodded at their père, though the man never looked Pascal's way. "Tell us of your journey, Père." His voice was tender, gentle. Revealing the heart of gold he tried to hide under a carefree and teasing manner.

Ro waited so long, she was almost certain he wasn't going to speak. But she also wasn't leaving the room until she heard his tale.

"When I got there, the ship's goods had been dispersed. The crew had split the large profit brought in and had gone in search of their homes."

"Large profit?"

"Without contacting you!"

Claude silenced his sisters with a look. Ro was glad. She was quite certain her fist would've caused more noise, not less.

"They thought me dead. Only the clerk at the shipping yard knew of my whereabouts, and he said he was too afraid to say anything because of how desperate the people were for the goods."

Another sister opened her mouth, but Claude quelled her with a fierce look. Bravo. Ro silently cheered him on. Now he just needed to direct that look at the lot of them to make them mind.

"I tried to track them down, but people are fearful. Willing to kill for a crust of bread. So, after several months, without any luck at all, I set off for home. A storm such as I've never seen arose, and I sought shelter."

Ro wondered how a voice could sound so dead when so many words were pouring from it. More words than he'd spoken in years. His eyes flew up and latched on to hers. Her breath caught at the intensity of it.

"I found a castle. In the woods."

Ro's heart skipped a beat. He *what*? Surely he hadn't said what she thought he had. Excitement filled her.

"Oui! Yes, I know! With eight turrets and a lined drive full of orange trees, bursting with blossoms and fruit. And the fireworks! Oh, it's so beautiful, isn't—"

Ro snapped her mouth closed. Everyone stared at her. She ducked her head, and her face filled with heat. Here came the teasing.

Père regarded her solemnly. "Oui. Beautiful. And it rose out of the mist, absent one moment and there the next, just as you said."

Ro soaked in his words, for once not feeling as if she were losing her sanity as everyone said. Someone else had seen it. Someone else had seen it! Her heart beat wildly.

"A castle? What do you mean there was a castle in the woods? What castle?"

More than one person shushed Bernadette this time.

"The minute I stepped through the gates, the storm abated. Snuffed out like a candle." His eyes drifted away. "Such loveliness. Such wealth! I was well taken care of." He moaned. "Oh, the meals! Such rich food as I haven't tasted in an age. I stayed until I felt like myself again, then I sought out my kind host. Finding no one, I was certain the castle was meant for me, and I was determined to claim it for us all."

Reinette interrupted, her voice small as she trembled under the combined glare of her brothers. "Dearest Père, could it have been a dream?"

He was quiet a moment, and Ro shot her a "thanks a lot" look. Fortunately, he started to speak again.

"I wondered that myself. How could anything so beautiful be real?"

Ro's eyes widened. They'd said she was crazy for being able to see it! But she could. Had been able to for a long time. Well, since it had disappeared. Now Père had seen it. That's why she dragged Cosette into the woods every year. It came to life at night, then dispersed with the rising of the sun. She would dream of happier times. And wish for the prince. Wonder what had happened to him. Why he wasn't helping her people.

But…the castle, though beautiful still, was only a shadow of its former glory. Yet no one believed her, no one remembered the strong prince and the kind king and queen who had once ruled. She was left to wonder if it was all a fantasy she had made up in her head.

But no. The memories were too real.

And somehow the entire kingdom had forgotten they once had a ruler.

"As I was leaving, I found a rose." He nodded to the flower still clutched in Ro's hand, and she looked at it for the first time. She gasped. She'd never seen a lovelier rose! White, impossibly glimmering as with a hidden light, lush and full of life, as large as her brother's hands side by side. Never had she seen something this beautiful, even when roses still grew in France.

"A—a terrible, monstrous beast sprang at me. Told me I would die for stealing his rose."

Cosette gasped, and each of her sisters looked stricken. Ro tensed. Well, that had done it. Any hope Ro had held that her sisters would believe she saw a castle in the woods vanished. She could see it in their eyes. Perhaps he'd been too long in the woods, out in the cold. Perhaps he'd had a monstrous dream. Perhaps his sanity was slipping. Ro's shoulders sagged.

But still—there was a beast in the castle? Was that why the prince had never been heard from or seen again?

"Surely he was dreaming?" Yvette whispered. Reinette ignored her.

"I begged for my life, told him of our plight, and…h-he told me—" He trembled and placed his hands over his face. "Oh, mon Dieu! What have I done?"

"There, there, dear Père!" Cosette rushed forward and put her arms around him. She lifted tear-filled eyes to Ro as if to ask what to do.

Ro shook her head. She had no idea.

"The horrid beast told me I had to give one of my daughters' lives in exchange for the flower. Only then could I repay my theft. Only then would I stop a-a *curse* from befalling our family."

The color drained from Ro's face, leaving her feeling light-headed. Another curse?

Claude and Pascal stiffened instantly. Pascal was quick with a response. "We won't let that happen, Père. You can count on it."

But Père once again acted as if he were alone in the room, talking to himself. "I tried to give it back. At least, I think I did. He wouldn't take it. Only told me to go and bring her back with me. Soon. It was soon, wasn't it? He laughed at me, didn't he? Or was it a woman? I swear I heard a woman laughing…"

Cosette and Ro stared at each other, eyes wide. What could they do? Could they believe any part of his tale? Ro glanced back at Père, and his eyes sought hers. She jolted at the force of his gaze.

"And the daughter to whom I gave it would pay the price."

All feeling abandoned her, leaving her numb. Had she truly heard him?

"You must go to the castle, little Rose. You must pay my debt. You are the only one who can stop the curse. It is written in the stars."

Ro jerked back as if she'd been slapped.

Fury glimmered in Pascal's eyes. "We *won't* let that happen." His words were a promise. Ro shot him a grateful look, then her stunned gaze returned to Père.

She opened her mouth to ask a question, but his eyes drifted away, and he was lost to them all, unmoved by further questioning.

Cosette cried out, and Yvette burst into tears, followed soon by the twins. Her brothers shouted, protesting, declaring Ro would never go, but it all faded away. Ro stared at the rose in her hands, oblivious to the noise, and wondered what in all the realms he could mean.

Then rage filled her. Rage such as she'd never felt.

How dare her père bargain his life for hers? No one controlled her destiny. Not her père, not the stars, not a magical beast, not some flower, not any *curse*. She crushed the rose in her hands, the thorns pricking her palms until blood dripped on the carpet.

"Rose?" Cosette's voice was filled with enough alarm to penetrate the haze she floated in.

"Non."

The noise in the room ceased. Ro turned to face Père.

"Non."

His dull eyes met hers, and she continued, whether he heard or not.

"I owe you nothing. I will not pay your debt, I will not be your scapegoat, I will not allow you to hurt us any longer."

Silence for a heartbeat.

He stood and slapped her. "How dare you."

Ro blinked, the pain crushing her heart more vibrant than the thorns embedded in her palm. She shook her head, trying to convince herself it hadn't just happened. To convince herself he still loved her. Fear crashed all around her, and she couldn't think. Couldn't fathom what had just happened. He'd never struck her before. Not once.

Père took her hands, gentling his tone. "You must. Don't you see, child? You will curse us all! There was magic in that castle such as I've never felt before. What do you think will happen if I do not fulfill my promise? You must go."

"Non, mon père. You cannot mean it. You don't mean it."

"I do, and you will." He grasped her shoulders, tightly. Pascal stepped forward, then hesitated. Père leaned close, and Ro's only thought was how bony his fingers felt now. How thin he was. "Don't you see? You can save us all! He will not kill me. He will not curse your sisters. We can live!"

"Do you call this living?" Ro shook her head, eyes wide, feeling all but five years old again. She would save them, but not how he wanted. "Non."

He shoved her away, and Ro stumbled, catching herself from falling by grabbing his chair. Instantly, Pascal's arm came about her shoulders and Claude stood close to her other side, one hand on her arm. Something filled Père's face that crushed Ro more than his slap, his neglect, or his words. Hate.

"Then you are dead to me. Get out of my sight." He turned and headed to his study. He paused and pointed one finger at her. "Don't come in my house again. You are not welcome here." Then he slammed the door behind him.

Ro touched her fingertips to the throbbing welt on her cheek.

Claude's voice was raspy. "Surely he didn't mean it."

"Curse us? What does he mean she will curse us?" one of her sisters wailed.

Cosette reached for her, sobbing. "Rosette…"

Ro shrugged off her brothers' touch and fled. Out the door, over the fence, across the field. And she didn't stop running as heavy snowflakes began pelting her from the sky.

6

o dropped to the ground, sucking in breaths. Even though she couldn't breathe, she began sobbing, only there wasn't enough air to do both. She cried and cried, whimpering, trying to get enough oxygen to her air-starved lungs.

She cried for her mère. Her père. Her sisters and brothers. Her Cosette. She sobbed for everything she'd known and everything she'd lost. She cried until she couldn't cry anymore and found herself staring up at the sky, the frigid breeze gentle in the barren branches for once, snowflakes collecting on her eyelashes. Her breath poofed in silent clouds above her face.

"Oh, Mère, how I wish you were here." She hiccupped between words. "Père would've never done such a thing."

She sat up, black leaves sticking to the side of her face and hair, and began shivering uncontrollably. She'd forgotten how cold it was. Though she was certain the trembling wasn't only from the temperature.

She'd been betrayed in the worst way, and by the one who should've protected her. Loved her. By the one she'd once treasured as Mère had. Had he ever even treasured her? His own

43

daughter? Oui. Long ago. Now hate filled the oft-vacant eyes where love and tenderness once resided.

She shook her head, desperate to quiet the thoughts that plagued her. Where was she? She glanced around, her breaths shuddering. Her eyes riveted on a familiar gate, a long, winding drive disappearing into overgrown trees. Her old house lay beyond, out of sight. How in all the realms had she run so far?

She eased forward and reached out a hand, then froze. She couldn't. Not after what she'd just lost. Too many painful memories were buried there.

She eased away from her former home, where she'd been so happy with Mère—where they'd all been so happy—and slipped back into the trees.

Her footsteps swiftly took her to a spot more familiar than any other place she knew. Her treehouse. Supposedly built for her brothers, Ro had made more use of it than they had.

It was her hiding place. Her sanctuary.

Her hands remembered the handholds without her having to remind them, and she scaled the tree, soon settling inside the structure. She looked around in awe and swiped bits of bark from her hands. Just as she'd left it. Frozen in time. She fingered the heavy pelt left there for late nights and chill weather.

Resolution filled her. There was but one path left to her now.

She would hunt wolves. And she would find the Mesdemoiselles of the Mountain, first chance she got. She'd heard the rumors since they'd first offered food to her starving village, though even she admitted she didn't pay as much attention as she ought. How could she? Her head was nearly always filled with the latest book she'd immersed herself in. But she'd heard enough.

They lived on a mountain and granted wishes. Yet their dwelling couldn't be found, not unless the Mesdemoiselles allowed it. Then they would grant one wish to the person desperate enough to find them.

And Ro would be that person. And she would become the best huntress this land had ever known, better than any of the huntsmen.

All of a sudden, her eyelids were too heavy to keep open. Without really thinking about it, she pulled the pelt over her shoulders, lay on her side, and slept.

&

"Ro? Ro, wake up. Ro!"

Someone prodded her side. Ro bolted up, eyes wide, senses reeling, trying to focus.

"Geez, it's just us, mon chou."

"Yeah, you look crazy enough to scare a rabbit."

One of them poked the pelt. "Non, a wolf."

"Non, a whole pack of wolves."

Her brothers snickered. Ro rolled her eyes.

"What do you want?"

Their laughter faded, replaced by the most somber expressions she'd seen on their faces. Ro realized with a jolt that that look had always been present, only they tried to cover it with mirth. She shivered as the wolf's pelt slid down her shoulders, revealing the threadbare dress beneath.

"We thought you might come here," Pascal said quietly, slipping off his jacket and wrapping it around her.

Claude nodded. "Yeah. You okay?"

Ro just stared at them, feeling completely dead inside. "What do you think."

Pascal winced. Claude glanced away.

"I'm sorry." She rubbed a hand over her face. "It's not your fault."

Pascal's look was fierce. "We won't let him take you, you know."

Her half-smirk didn't reach her eyes, though her heart melted a little. "I know."

"Do you still want to go with the Mesdemoiselles of the Mountain?" Claude asked.

Ro blinked, her mind thrown into another whirlwind. *Oui! Ah, oui.* She nodded.

"Good." Pascal dropped a satchel she hadn't noticed he carried in front of her. "They'll be here today."

Ro blinked again. It seemed the only thing she could do when stuff was thrown at her at such a rapid-fire pace.

"Stop doing that. You look like a scared rabbit."

Her face flushed, and she scowled. "Doing what?"

"Yeah, that scared-rabbit blink you've got." Claude snickered again.

"Rabbits don't blink, you idiot," Ro growled.

"They do too. And they look just as stupid as you do."

"Shut up!"

"Pay attention!" Pascal didn't care to be sidetracked, though he had no problem doing it to others. "Everyone will be gone today—Cosette plans on using all those livres—the ones you left *us*, by the way."

Ro shrugged. "Sorry. I'll get you more."

Claude nudged her and winked. "You'd better."

Surely he was joking? Ro couldn't tell.

Pascal continued as if they hadn't spoken. "And the girls are mad for shopping, so you can sneak back in and get anything we missed." He nodded at the bag.

"Yeah, we didn't want to touch your unmentionables," Claude cut in.

They both guffawed this time.

"Get on with it," Ro growled, her face once again feeling uncomfortably hot.

Pascal shrugged. "Père has left again, so we'll get the girls away—"

"I want to see Cosette."

"—except for Cosette—"

"And I don't want her to know I'm leaving."

"—and we won't say a word about you leaving. Geez, is that all?" Pascal looked cross again.

Ro smiled innocently at him. "That's all."

They nodded and opened the trapdoor in the middle of the floor. Claude pushed the rope ladder out, and it swung crazily as he stepped down on the first rung.

Claude pointed at the bag. "Oh, and use some tooth powder. Cause, woo-ie, do you need it."

Ro tried to smack him, but Claude scurried down and disappeared, his laughter ringing in the trees. Pascal chortled, blocking her swing at him. He stepped onto the ladder but paused, his head and shoulders still in the treehouse. That serious look crept back on his face, and Ro's heart dropped. Would she see them again?

After a moment's hesitation, he reached into his pocket and produced the rose. Ro gasped, another sucker punch to her gut. It was just as lush and beautiful as when she'd first seen it, not crushed in the least, and the white flower stilled glowed with an inner light. He held it out to her.

"Get rid of it," she hissed.

Hurt flashed on his face, but he covered it quickly. "I think you're going to need this."

She shook her head. "Non."

He gently laid it before her. "Just think about it. I can't explain it, but you need this flower, especially if you seek the Mesdemoiselles of the Mountain." He shrugged. "Maybe you can trade it for their help."

She just looked at him.

"Be there as soon as you can. I can't guarantee Père won't be back."

Ro nodded, her jaw tight. "You can count on it."

7

———————

Claude stood in the yard with a rake. Of course he wasn't using it. Just leaning on it while he watched for Père's return. Ro shook her head. Typical.

Ro waited behind the stable. "Ro. My name is Ro," she muttered to herself.

Today was the day. The day she would leave her village, Rose no more. Ro, a strong, vibrant huntress who answered to no man.

Pascal left their house and hurried toward her, Cosette at his side. He waved Cosette on and stayed in front of the barn, where he could easily see the other side of the cottage.

Ro frowned. Père must've unnerved them all last night.

"Rose!" Cosette flung herself at her sister and held on tight. "Oh, I am so sorry. Are you okay?" She pulled back and searched Ro's eyes.

"I'm fine." She tried to smile, but it stuck somewhere in her throat, and she swallowed hard instead. "Really, I'm fine."

"No, you're not." Her voice turned soft. "He should've never hit you."

Ro's eyes turned flinty. "No, he shouldn't have."

49

Cosette's sympathy instantly turned to concern. "What will you do?"

Ro shrugged and looked away.

"I see."

Ro glanced back, alarmed. Did she?

A bright smile replaced Cosette's frown. "I'm sure Père didn't mean it. He must've been tired from his trip. Disheartened. We'll just talk to him. He'll apologize. You'll see."

Ro shook her head. Wasn't that just like Cosette to see the bright side of everything?

Cosette squeezed her hand. "Wait here. I'll go get the baskets." She hurried toward the little cottage.

Ro followed her sister's every step with her eyes, soaking her in. Memorizing every detail. She shook herself from staring once Cosette disappeared around the corner. She took a deep breath and leaned against the barn, closing her eyes.

"I'm Ro. Ro. Bonjour, my name is Ro. Nice to meet you. I'm Ro." She groaned. She needed to sound strong, confident, not like she was scared out of her mind. She squared her shoulders and stared at the stone fence bordering their property. "Bonjour. I'm Ro. Huntress. Hunter. Of things."

Someone bumped her shoulder. "Just keep talking to yourself, mon chou. People will think you're as crazy as Madame Savon."

She gasped and jerked toward the voice. "Claude! Aren't you keeping watch?"

He shrugged. "It's more entertaining to watch you talk to yourself."

"I am *not* talking to myself."

Claude raised an eyebrow, and his eyes blazed with mirth. "Oh? Perhaps you *should* take Madame Savon's place. Before people start to talk…and things."

She slugged his arm and started to give a sharp retort, but Cosette was back, smiling at her, two large baskets over both arms. "Of course they won't. She's a dear."

Claude snorted.

The tiniest smile materialized on Ro's face.

Cosette waved, her movement hampered by the baskets. "I've got to get there before all the goods are gone. See you when we get back from the village!" Her eyes held a promise. "We'll talk then."

Ro held her smile in place by the sheerest of willpower. *No, we won't.*

The smile vaporized the moment Cosette's back was turned. Ro watched Cosette, flanked by Claude and Pascal, walk away. Pascal glanced back at Ro, brow scrunched, eyes sad. Ro gave a firm nod. He sighed and turned back around, and the three disappeared around the bend.

Her eyes sought the void where the castle should have been. "Give me strength," she prayed to no one in particular. Maybe the Creator still heard her. Maybe not.

She darted inside. She gathered what she needed quickly, before her sisters came back and Père caught her in his home. If he even bothered returning from his aimless wanderings. One thing was certain: she wouldn't be coming back.

She took a leather strap and tied back her hair. She changed into her brother's trousers, grabbed Père's old crossbow, and stuffed anything else she needed in the bag her brothers had given her. Then she took the same trail as her siblings, soon gaining on them in her haste.

She crouched behind a cluster of barrels—once holding the finest wine in France, now cracked and dry—and waited until her siblings were done at the market and heading home. The rest of the square bustled with townspeople trading much-needed goods with each other.

Cosette's voice rang out, and Ro tucked herself tighter into her hiding spot.

"Can you believe it? Look at all we were able to buy! Wait till Rose sees!"

Ro peeked as her sister pranced past her, capturing the joy

on her sister's face in her memory forever. "I will never forget you," she whispered.

Soon Cosette's happy chattering faded and disappeared entirely.

Ro took a deep breath, stood, and made her way to the Mesdemoiselles' wagon. Her heart clenched at the thought of having to face the three women. They made her skin crawl. But Cosette was worth it. She glanced up and froze. An old man, tall and still full of vibrant life, though his hair was peppered with gray, handed out vegetables in the Mesdemoiselles' place.

She blinked. Who was he?

She waited, invisible in the crush of villagers whose only goal was to trade for enough food to last until the Mesdemoiselles' wagon came again. But where were they?

Not one appeared. Just the old man, working by himself. Someone called him "wagon master." Ro took a deep breath. Then he was the one she needed to ask.

Ro made her way forward, slipping through the throng, and stood tall before him. She met his eyes without a flinch.

"I wish to see the Mesdemoiselles of the Mountain."

She expected the wagon master to object. He simply eyed her for the briefest of seconds, then jerked his grizzled head toward the covered wagon. "Get in." He continued wordlessly distributing vegetables in exchange for any valuable the people of Champagne had left.

Ro swallowed and peeked inside the enclosed wagon, expecting to be greeted by the haggard women she so loathed to see. Nothing. Just vegetables, lush and ripe. Apparently she was going to see the Mesdemoiselles elsewhere.

She slipped past the mounds of food and settled in the ever-widening empty spot, thankful the flaps would hide her should her sister decide to come back. While she waited, her gaze strayed to the castle, where it should've peeked through the flaps. She moved one aside to see better.

Nothing. She settled back to wait. And hide. Her eyelids grew heavy.

She jolted awake, and the wagon dipped, swaying gently as it rumbled away from her village. Moonlight beamed brightly all around the wagon, but the noises of trade and haggling had died away. The castle, glaring white in the vibrant moonlight, arrested her full attention.

She wanted to capture the sight forever, but the desire to do so slipped away. The prince hadn't saved them. Père hadn't rescued her. The Creator hadn't restored her mère or her land. She was leaving her home, the sister she loved, to track wolves like a common huntsman. Her jaw clenched.

But wait. How could she see the castle again so soon? It hadn't been a year yet.

A voice whistled through the trees, carried on the breeze. "Huntresssss..."

She jolted awake, the noise of trade drowning out the dream. Murky light from an overcast sky greeted her, and she peeked out of the flaps. Still in her village. Still daytime. Yet the horror of that one word stayed with her. She eased back into her spot. Chatter came and drifted away as customers procured their coveted goods.

No matter that it had been a dream, every bit of it was true. She could trust no one but herself.

She had no idea how long she sat there and seethed, but the wagon master soon emptied his wagon of vegetables, now piled high with furniture and trinkets instead, climbed into the seat, and set the cart in motion.

Anger slid through her as the towering castle in her mind faded from view. She would never wait for someone else to rescue her. She would never wait for a prince to save her, not again.

She would never be helpless. She would become the huntress, Ro, and she'd be good at it. A town crier thundered through the village, shouting something about a Gautier, though Ro couldn't make out what. Cheers followed the announcement.

The cart exited the village, rocking from side to side to the cries of "Gautier! Gautier will save us!" Ro clutched the sides of the wagon as it swayed. Gautier be hanged—whoever he was. She couldn't escape fast enough.

&.

Ro tossed in her sleep. She knew she was asleep. She knew she dreamed. But no matter how hard she tried, she just couldn't wake up.

She fought harder.

Three witches on broomsticks circled her, black cloaks flapping in the wind. Their screeches and laughter filled the air; they laughed at her. They were bent on tormenting her. And Ro had no idea why.

Ro had never been so terrified in her life. Yet she still couldn't make herself wake up.

Ro stood frozen below them as they circled her, taunting her. Their twisted faces, vicious sneers, and hate-filled eyes washed over her, and her knees shook. Why couldn't she move?

Then the first dove at her. She had just enough time to see the second and third follow their leader before she turned and fled.

She could move. Finally!

She ran and ran, but she never covered any distance.

Something hit her from behind, and she slammed into the ground.

"Non!" she cried.

"Yes..." a wicked voice hissed in her ear.

She tried to scramble to her feet, but a broom handle pinned her to the ground. Two more swiftly followed.

The more she struggled, the more they laughed. Her back ached so, so much.

Ro was too scared to sob, too frightened to make a noise. She opened her mouth in a silent scream and clawed to get away.

She was flipped roughly to her back. She stared into the faces of her assailants. Black crept through their veins. A gray hue overtook their decaying features, features straight from a nightmare. Black teeth, black nails, black eyes. Hatred spilled from them, directed solely at her, as spittle flew out of hissing mouths and gnashing teeth.

Why did they hate her so much? She didn't understand.

One of them leaned forward, and Ro tried with all her might to press herself into the ground.

"Now that we have found you, Huntress, we will not let you escape. You will die!"

They flew at her as one, black claws and deadened fingers outstretched, reaching for her face to tear her apart.

8

———

o's head cracked against the side of the wagon, and she woke with a gasp. The wagon jerked crazily as it settled to an abrupt halt. She bolted upright. Where was she? When had she fallen asleep?

Oh, all the saints above, that *dream*! She rubbed her arms, trying desperately to erase the images from her mind, but they continued to swirl around her memories and haunt her.

The wagon seat creaked, and heavy boots hit the earth with a *thump*, then pounded toward her.

She scrambled down the bed of the wagon to the back and jumped over the edge, landing with a jolt. Her wide eyes met those of the wagon master's. He nodded past her, then turned and started tying back the flaps to the wagon's canvas walls.

Ro cautiously peeked behind her, then forgot everything else.

So much green. Everywhere. It filled her senses until she could almost taste it. Grass, shrubs, hedges, trees. The soft rustle of leaves danced in the wind. Sunlight streamed through the branches bursting with life, warming her face. She was in a haven not known since the prince had left his people to fend off a curse they knew nothing of. Oh, the greenery!

And sunlight! Bright, blazing, yellow gloriousness.

Not the muggy fog that permeated her entire existence—since that day. The day the world had stopped, gray had invaded the sky, and black had overrun the green.

She barely heard his heavy boots circle the wagon to the other side.

Tears wanted to fill her eyes, but she couldn't find the strength to call them forth. She took a deep breath and just enjoyed the sweetness of it all.

A horse shifted, leather creaked, and Ro jerked back to her surroundings. The wagon still stood beside her, and she still didn't know where she was.

She edged around the wagon, afraid to touch it and awaken from the first lovely dream she'd had since Mère died. The ancient wagon driver, his back to Ro, stood talking to a goddess, a woman so lovely she couldn't be of this world. Tall, stately, dressed in deep-red velvet, hair black as midnight, falling to her waist in rich, undulating silk. Her very presence filled the air around Ro and commanded her attention. Who was she?

Where were the Mesdemoiselles of the Mountain?

They were old, ugly, terrifying, and held all of France in their arthritic hands.

Ro stilled. The dream. She shook her head and laughed. She'd been so terrified to speak with them again, her dreams had made them into witches. She chuckled at herself, crossed her arms, and leaned against the wagon, waiting for the wagon master to finish his conversation so they could continue on to the Mesdemoiselles of the Mountain.

As though the woman had heard her thoughts, her eyes left the wagon master's face and latched on to Ro—eyes dark and fathomless, skin, flawless. She smiled with blood-red lips and beckoned Ro forward. "Come, ma fille."

Ro straightened and took a hesitant step forward, once again overcome by the lush greenery behind the woman. A garden. A real one. Filled with vegetables. Beautiful, lush, glowing vegetables. Ro's mouth dropped open, and her eyes shot to the woman in the clearing.

"You grow all this food?"

The woman grinned, lovely, yet…not. "You could say that."

"But how — why — how?"

The woman winked at her. "Magic."

Ro shook her head. She needed to untie her tongue this instant. Well, what she really needed was Cosette. She always knew exactly what to say and in the loveliest way possible. Ro straightened and pulled back her shoulders. She'd have to do.

She met the woman's eyes boldly. "May I see the Mesdemoiselles of the Mountain?"

The woman's smile crawled through Ro's belly and made everything vile come to life. Ro refused to squirm. The woman nodded, as regal as any courtier. "At your service, Mademoiselle."

"Y-you?"

The woman winked. "Oui. I'm the only Mademoiselle of this Mountain, in fact."

The woman's image wavered, and a hint of the pasty, frail creature that had visited her village before peeked through. Yet there was something else Ro couldn't quite grasp… At once Ro was back in her dream, being tortured by three witches. The woman before her, one of them.

She snapped back to reality, gasping for breath. "You're a witch?" she demanded, her voice more breathless than she would've liked.

The woman smiled, her beautiful visage wavering between bliss and all things hideous. "Oui."

"And you are the only one?" That couldn't be right. Ro had seen three. There were three of them. And they were haggard and ugly. Who was this woman? "What happened to the others?"

Her smile turned positively giddy, her voice filled with delight. "I killed them."

The witch's laugh sent shudders vibrating up and down Ro's form. "You—you wouldn't."

Her eyes darted to the wagon master. He now unloaded the cart, not a change to his expression. He retrieved a small chest from under the wagon seat and carried it inside a house set behind the garden.

"Oh, but I did. Then I ate them."

Ro took a step back, her face twisting in revulsion. Any desire to ask anything of this woman shriveled up and died. She'd rather ask the huntsmen in her village.

And that wasn't going to happen.

The woman stalked toward her, the cadence of her words low, rumbling, exquisite, and Ro very much felt like prey. "You know how it is with sisters. Can't stand them, wish to be rid of them, then *poof*"—she stopped just in front of her and made an exploding motion with her hands—"it's done. No more troublesome, petty, nagging, grasping sisters. You know how it is, don't you?"

The Mademoiselle's eyes bored into her very soul.

Ro hesitated as an unholy desire unfurled inside of her. The woman's words actually tempted her. It was what she wished for night and day—to be rid of her sisters. All but one. Her stomach clenched, and she hated herself. What she'd wished for and what this woman had done were but a breath away. Ro feared this is what she'd become if she let hatred lead her.

The burning, broiling hatred that had consumed her since her life had spiraled out of control.

Ro shook her head furiously. "No, never. I would never—" No matter how many times she'd wished to be rid of them, she'd never kill them. Or eat them. What in all the realms?

"Oh? Never? Not any of your five sisters who refuse to work? Refuse to help? Those who pick on the youngest—"

Ro shuddered violently and threw her hands up, slamming her thoughts to emptiness.

"Oh. You can block me?"

I what?

"I see. It is no matter. I will learn her name soon enough. No mortal can withstand me." She turned and flounced back toward the wagon. "Fill it to the rim, Hamish! The towns-people are desperate for my goods." She turned and smiled at Ro. "No matter where they come from."

Ro had to get out of here. Now.

She turned to run down the road they'd just traveled, but the wagon master was there, blocking her.

He nodded toward the house, wordlessly, right past the large burn pile he'd been heaving furniture into.

Ro didn't know what to do. So she turned and made her way to the house, her heart beating wildly. What made her obey?

Her trembling knees and fear-wracked heart, that's what. Why, oh why hadn't she stayed in her village?

The Mademoiselle of the Mountain fell in step behind her, and Ro's back crawled with the thought of that woman's gaze upon her.

She glanced back once. The Mademoiselle of the Mountain smiled, a cunning, vicious thing, teeth stunningly white against too-red lips. Ro spun back around and marched forward, the wagon master close behind.

She passed someone in the garden, someone she hadn't seen before. Thin, scrawny, with a shock of vibrant orange hair, the lanky lad took a moment from his hoeing to stare at her, eyes the size of silver livres.

Help me, she mouthed.

Fear flashed on his face. He glanced behind her and ducked his head, working feverishly on his row.

Ro's heart sank even further. She should've known. She couldn't rely on anyone but herself.

Her eyes glinted as she got closer to the dwelling. She would escape, she would become a huntress on her own, without the witch's help, and Cosette would never want for anything ever again.

And she wouldn't give in to whatever the witch wanted, no matter what.

Ro stepped inside the dwelling and spun to face the door. The wagon master stood back, allowing the witch to enter, then closed the door. His footsteps thudded away.

The Mademoiselle of the Mountain smiled at her, sending shivers all up and down Ro's spine, and moved to the wood-burning stove along one wall. She stirred something bubbling in a mid-sized cauldron on the stove.

Ro blinked. She thought witches belonged in stories, wild tales, not real life.

"Now, what you've come to ask me and what you're going to ask me are two completely different things. So ask it."

Ro blanched. No way. Not ever. Not as long as she lived.

She crossed her arms and lifted her chin, offering the witch her haughtiest glare.

The witch chuckled, her back to Ro. "I can't do anything without your asking it, you know."

She poured the bubbling brew into two mugs and settled them on a tray, then filled a cup with real sugar and poured lovely, white, silky cream into a small service. Ro's mouth watered. The witch settled the tray on a table set between two overstuffed chairs and motioned for Ro to join her.

"Please sit."

Ro's boots padded over the deep-red area rug covering the ash-colored planks of the floor. Ro wanted to lose herself in the luxury of her surroundings, small though the cabin was, but instead stayed focused on her host.

Ro settled into the chair offered her and waited. She ignored the teacup. No way was she drinking it, sugar and cream notwithstanding. She wasn't about to be poisoned or have a spell placed on her somehow.

The witch nodded at her and took a sip from her cup. "Proceed."

"I'd rather leave, thank you very much."

"But you can't. Don't you listen to gossip, chérie?"

Ro's brows furrowed. What on earth was she talking about?

The witch's teeth gleamed in the dim light of the interior of the cabin. "You should pay more attention. You've sought the Mesdemoiselles of the Mountain." Her smile stretched wider. "Well, the Mademoiselle of the Mountain, for quite some time now, actually."

Ro's stomach sickened. What in the realms had she been thinking, seeking a witch's help? She may not be on speaking terms with the Creator, but seeking the help of someone who so blatantly hated Him was crossing so many lines.

She was an idiot.

"In order for you to leave, you must ask what you came to ask and accept whatever help I give." She nodded toward the front window. "Or you have to stay and help me for the rest of your days, like that poor fellow." She shook her head and sighed. "It was such a simple thing I asked. Can you believe he didn't want to bring me his sister's still-beating heart?"

Ro gagged and clamped her hand over her mouth. The

handful of radishes the wagon master had given her were going to stay down. They were.

The witch smiled, taking her time to lift the cup to her lips. "Ask away, my dear. I have no more need of a beating heart. Not yet, anyway. My face is still young enough to please me. Or would you rather stay?"

Her face what? Ro's jaw clenched. "I'm not staying, and I'm not asking anything of you. Not after what you've done."

The witch's smile grew impossibly bright. "Oh, but you will. Do you know how I know that?"

Ro shook her head. She didn't care. She just wanted out. But she was terrified of standing up to the witch, and she hated herself for it.

"Desperation has a certain stench to it."

"I'm not desperate."

"No? You're here, aren't you?"

Ro's heart sank. She was. With shaking hands, all thoughts of being a huntress forgotten, she reached into her brother's jacket and withdrew the white rose, still as exquisite as the day Père had given it to her, even though she'd both crushed it and slept on it. It gave off a slight glow, lighting the cabin with warmth and a sense of peace.

The witch's smile froze, and Ro could've sworn fear flashed across her face, as swift and fleeting and violent as lightning.

"Where did you get that?" she whispered.

"My père traded me for it."

The witch's eyes stayed glued on the flower, though she made no move to take it. "And why do you offer it to me now?"

Ro had no idea. None. She just wanted out, to be rid of the blasted thing, to be away from this place.

"Ask me," the witch growled.

Ro jumped and stammered, "I-I wanted you to take it from me, I guess. I wanted to know if—if the promise holds. If I have to go." *But I'm not asking anything of you. Really!* The protest stuck in her throat.

The Mademoiselle nodded slowly. "All right. I will take it from you. In exchange, I give you your freedom, from here and the promise of which you cannot speak, the promise to the beast"—Ro's eyes flashed. How did she know that?—"food for your family as long as they all shall live"—which might not be very long if the witch had anything to do with it—"and your return to your père's graces."

Warmth seeped into Ro for the first time since coming to this place. The witch could do that?

The Mademoiselle smiled, her carefree manner returning. "Of course I can do that, ma fille." She winked. "I might even throw in a touch of respect from your sisters."

Now she knew the witch was lying. That was impossible.

"Put the flower down."

Ro followed the witch's nod and set it on the tray that still held the steaming mugs. The witch took a full breath once she did so, and without moving, seemed to put as much distance between herself and the pulsating flower as possible.

"All I ask is one teensy tiny favor in return."

Ro stiffened. "And what is that?"

She leaned forward, eyes glowing with an unholy light. "The Fairy Queen's head."

"Her *what*?" First witches, now fairies? The beast, she accepted. Somehow. The curse, she'd lived with it for fifteen years. But this, this she couldn't handle. "What Fairy Queen?"

The Mademoiselle of the Mountain huffed. "You carry one of her flowers, stupid girl. You'll need it to gain entrance into her realm."

Ro just stared at her. She was insane. Completely, utterly insane.

The witch started muttering to herself, confirming it. "Of course not her heart—they wouldn't let me have that. It would disappear the moment you cut it out of her. But her head... now *that* they would not expect." Her smile grew, and her focus returned to Ro. "I want it on a platter."

"Never." Ro's voice erupted from her in a strangled whisper. She strengthened it. "Never." She didn't care whether this queen was real or not; she was not bringing the witch anyone's head. Ugh.

"Oh, but you will. You haven't the power to resist me, little one. Those who can are few and far between, especially once I place a compulsion spell on you."

"You won't. You can't. I won't let you." Ro had never felt this level of tangy, coppery fear before. It ate away at her insides, turning her into a quivering mess of cowardice.

"And the best part?" The witch smiled. "You won't remember any of this. And you'll wonder what beastly devil possessed you to do what I ask of you."

The witch's laughter rang through the cottage while Ro's heart shriveled and dropped past the floor. *Creator, help me!*

The witch rose slowly, drawing out the moment, her smile letting Ro know how much she enjoyed it. She started muttering nonsensical words—Latin, Ro's brain told her past all the screaming it was doing—and a ball of light appeared in her hands, growing as she muttered. She roughly turned her words to French. "I compel you! Do as I say, return with the Queen of the Fairies' head, and remember none of it."

She thrust her hands out at Ro, and the power with it.

Ro yelped and jumped to her feet. "Stop!"

The power wrapped around her, embracing her yet not touching her, as if an invisible shield held it at bay, then shot back to the witch. She screamed, her hands blazing with fire.

Thunder crackled outside and shook the house. Lightning flashed and lit every corner of the dark room. It wasn't as clean as it appeared. A tingle started in Ro's scalp and slowly consumed her body. Buzzing filled her ears.

The witch plunged her hands into the mugs' bubbling brew, then froze, mouth open, eyes wide. She shut her mouth and fixed the worst glare Ro had ever seen on her. "Hamish!"

The door bounced open, the sharp noise covered by

another crackle of thunder. The wagon master's composure was completely gone, panic enveloping every bit of him. "A storm! Inside the grounds. That's never happened be—"

"So you bring me a huntress, do you?" She bounded across the room, streaming liquid behind her that sizzled once it hit the smooth planks, wrapped her hand around Hamish's throat, and lifted him clean off the floor. "Do you have a death wish, old man?"

Ro stumbled back. "Stop!"

The witch dropped him and spun to face her. "Careful with your words, girl. They have more power than you know." Ro's eyes widened the same time the witch's did, and the Mademoiselle clamped a blackened, blistering hand over her mouth. "Why did I say that?" She pointed a finger at Ro. Ro blinked. A finger that looked shriveled and-and *old* in the lightning flashes, not just burnt. The skin slowly knit back together and smoothed out. "You're making me say that, aren't you? Aren't you?"

Three more bright flashes followed the first.

Ro shook her head. "I'm not. Honest."

"Get out. Get out of my house!" the woman shrieked.

Ro lunged for the rose and fled. She cursed herself. Why on earth had she grabbed it? She flew out the open door, bounded down the trail—nearly trampling the working boy who was running from the storm, right in her way—and flew past the wagon. She slammed into something invisible and flew back. She hit the ground hard.

Ro sat up, rubbing her head. Thinking of the last time she'd hit her head. About three months ago. Saving Cosette. She blinked back tears. Would she ever see her sister again?

Laughter filled the air behind her. "Well, you aren't as powerful as I thought, ma chérie."

Ro stumbled to her feet and faced her enemy.

"You apparently belong to me now." The woman's smile broadened as she stalked toward her, hands now completely whole, though her face wasn't as young as it had been. "But I can't have you around, burning me at whim, bringing storms into my haven. Fear not, little huntress. I will put you out of your misery, then you will never have to be unhappy again." She raised her hands to the sky and uttered deep, dark words that filled Ro's soul with loathing and trembling.

Ro covered her ears, but it made no difference. The words snaked through her being and filled her with revulsion. Ro hunkered against the wagon and waited.

Nothing happened.

The witch paused, then repeated her strange-sounding words. She didn't raise her voice, but the timbre of her voice changed, going even lower.

Ro shuddered, tucking herself harder against the wagon wheel.

This time, panic lit the woman's eyes when nothing happened.

Ro frowned. What was she expecting to happen?

The woman starting speaking again, but with greater urgency. The words began to churn in Ro's gut, physically painful, and she had to keep herself from writhing on the ground.

"Stop, stop, stop!" Ro cried in agony.

Thunder rattled the carriage, and a bolt of lightning zapped the ground next to the witch's feet. She flew back, landing on her side. Her head whipped around, and she stared at Ro, hatred glimmering in her eyes.

Ro looked between the witch and roiling clouds above. She controlled the storm? But—how was that possible?

She stood to her feet, shaking, certain a random bolt of lightning would strike her next. She pointed a shaking finger at the witch.

She was going to provide for her sister, and no witch was going to stop her. And there was only one way to do that. Alive.

Ro shouted words that rose up in her being, coming from a place she didn't even know existed. "I command you in the name of the Creator to leave this place, never to return! You will not harm one more person! You will not curse one more person! You will not cause one more person to do terrible things, then forget why. You are *done*."

Lightning zapped around the witch, three strikes, three different places. She cried out and hunkered away from each one.

"Be gone, witch!"

The largest bolt of lightning Ro had ever seen lit up the ground where the witch had been standing. Ro stood there, mesmerized, not the least bit afraid. It arched and popped and hissed, just staying there.

Then it vanished. The storm faded.

The witch was gone.

10

Ro sank to the ground. *What just happened?* She didn't believe in the Creator. *Did she?*

Yet the words were not her own. She knew she had to say them, just as she knew she had to breathe. Without a thought.

Ro shook her head and staggered to her feet. Where the witch had been standing smoked, a burnt patch of grass the only sign someone had once stood there.

Ro gazed down at her shaking hands. *How had she done that? Obliterated the witch with one swipe of her palm? Where had the magic come from?*

Her hands shook even more violently.

Whooping penetrated her swirling thoughts, and she spun toward the noise. The wagon master, the quiet, stoic, never-made-a-sound wagon master danced behind her, cheering and throwing his hat into the air over and over.

"She's dead! By all the saints, you've done and killed that plague."

He broke into a jig that had the corner of Ro's mouth tilting upward. But only for a second.

"Please, don't tell anyone. I don't know how—"

"Don't tell anyone? You're dang-blasted off yer rocker if

you think I'm going to keep this to myself. You killed that viper! Of course I'm going to tell everyone."

He took off running, heading for the path that would lead him out of the woods and down the mountain.

Ro darted after him and raised one hand, hoping to stop him. "Wait!"

He slammed into an invisible force and fell back, dust poofing where he landed. Ro jerked still, mouth open.

He looked at her, eyes wide. "You-you're the new Mademoiselle of the Mountain. You're a witch!"

She snorted. "No, I'm not. Don't be ridiculous." She reached out a hand to help him up.

Fear filled his eyes, and he cowed away from her. "You've killed one terror, only to be the next. We'll never be free. Never!"

He curled into a ball, right there on the dirt road, and sobbed. Heat crawled up Ro's neck and set her face on fire. Now this was just embarrassing.

Ro rolled her eyes after the longest few seconds of her life. "Oh, for goodness sake." She crouched next to him and shook his shoulder. "Get up and knock it off. I'm no witch, and I have no intention of being a Mademoiselle of the Mountain. None. You have nothing to worry about."

He jerked away from her touch. "You don't get it, do you?" He nodded toward the invisible boundary. "No one leaves this place until they make a deal with the witch. The witch is dead, and you killed her. That makes you the new master of this place."

Ro stood, head reeling.

What could she possibly say to that?

But, if she was the new master of this place...ideas exploded in her head, pelting her a thousand at a time.

What she could do! Her people wouldn't starve. Cosette wouldn't starve. Ro would never have to rely on anyone but herself ever again. She could learn to hunt. Here.

She grabbed the man's shoulder again. "Get up!"

He stood and faced her, a measure of his dignity regained. Ro forgot herself and grasped both of his shoulders, tightly.

"Can you hunt?"

He nodded, eyes dead, face stoic, tear trails painting lines through the dirt on his face. "Yes, why?"

"Can you teach me?"

One eyebrow went up. "That is what you require of me?"

"What? No, not require. I'm asking. Will you teach me?"

"And once you learn, you will let me go? I'll be free?"

Ro scowled. What was it with this man's obsession that she owned him? "Since you won't believe me, yes, free, whatever. Will you?"

He looked resigned to his fate. "If that is what you require of me, then yes."

She nodded toward the wagon. "And will you still deliver the food?"

His quiet demeanor slipped over him like a mask. "Oui, Mademoiselle. And what of the boy?" He nodded behind her.

She glanced behind her. The redheaded lad stood behind her, hat in hand, trembling, dirt smudged across his cheek. He couldn't have been, what, more than fifteen?

"Oh." She turned to face him fully. "And what do you do?"

He wrung the hat in his hands. "Mostly tend the garden, draw water, start fires. Those sorts of things."

She nodded. "Right, then. Would you still be willing to do that?"

His eyes sought the man behind her, and she glanced between the two.

The lad swallowed hard. "What I'd really like, Mademoiselle, is to go home."

"Oh. Of course. I understand."

His eyes lit. "So I can go?"

She nodded. "Of course." She met their eyes straight on.

"You both can. But promise me you will not speak a word of what happened here."

The wagon master sniffed and turned away, jaw tight. He began loading the wagon with vegetables.

The boy ducked his head and walked forward, giving Ro a wide berth. As far as Ro was concerned, they were both being ridiculous.

Ro started to say something to the wagon master when the boy hit the invisible wall and flew back.

Ro stared, mouth open. "What on earth?"

The wagon master kept his back to her, but his voice was gruff, his tone hard. "It was as I told you. Only a witch can kill another witch. This cursed ground now belongs to you, and we are now your slaves instead of hers." His gaze pierced her. "Time will tell which of you is worse."

"Oh, for heaven's sake!" Ro stomped forward and pushed through the barrier. Not a tingle, not a zap, not a barrier. Not anymore. She spun around and put her hands on her hips. "I'm out. Now you try it." Neither male moved. "Come on! What are you waiting for? Surely if I'm out here, you can be as well?"

The wagon master moved forward and tapped the wall. It arched and popped and hissed. The boy didn't even try. Ro's heart dropped. It couldn't be.

"Mademoiselle, can you see the garden? The house?"

She glanced past him. "Of course. Why?"

His gaze was level. "Only the Mesdemoiselles could see through the enchantment."

Ro lifted her chin, refusing to believe it. "Oh, yeah? Then how can you find this place?"

"I am bound to go and return, as my master dictates."

Ro's shoulders slumped, and she trudged back to the other side of the so-called "barrier" this absurd man couldn't seem to cross. She rubbed her forehead. "Why can't you leave again?"

The wagon master shrugged. "We are the only two who

have refused the witch's bargain, and she couldn't place a spell on us to do her bidding. We are cursed to remain in the witch's employ until one, the curse is broken, or two, the witches all die."

His direct gaze when he said it chilled Ro to the core. Great, now she had two curses to worry about instead of just one. And possibly a knife in the back.

She swallowed hard, then gave them both her best glare. "Let's get a few things straightened out from the beginning. One, I am not a witch. Two, I don't want either of you as slaves, and I will do everything within my power to break this stupid curse over you."

She raised her hand, though neither had moved to interrupt her. She lowered her hand. She'd have to get used to not being around siblings who constantly interrupted her.

"Three, all I want is to feed my family and learn to hunt. That's it. That's why I came to see the Mesdemoiselles of the Mountain. I want to provide for myself, I want to break this curse over my country, and I want my people not to starve. Do we understand each other?"

The lad's eyes had brightened during her tirade, but the wagon master's had stayed dull and lifeless. Kind of like Père's. Her heart immediately went out to him and constricted painfully at the same time.

She implored him with a look. "I do not want to enslave you. I promise. If you help me, I will do everything within my power to set you free." She waved her hand to the path that led away from the cottage. "I would let you go right now if I could."

He didn't look convinced. "You'll need weapons."

Hope lit within her like a flame. "I have a crossbow in the wagon." And why was this the first time she'd remembered it?

He nodded. "It's a start." He turned his back and concentrated on his wagon once more.

The boy was eyeing her, but he ducked his head as soon as

she looked at him. He moved to go past her. She fell into step beside him, and neither said a word for a few paces. Once they were closer to the garden—and farther away from the wagon master, Ro noted—the boy spoke in a low, fervent voice.

"Did you mean what you said? About letting us go?"

Ro snorted. "Of course! I don't want to enslave anyone."

The boy studied her. "That's good. If you stay strong, fight for what you believe in, maybe you can beat this. Power is a heady thing, once you've experienced it."

Ro frowned and met his gaze. They stopped and stared at each other. Ro realized with a jolt that the lad feared for her. He was afraid she'd give in to whatever power had seduced the witch.

She nodded. "Then I'll need your help, um—what was your name again?"

He grinned, a toothy but winsome thing. "Clement."

"Clement. I'll need your help then. Think you can do that?"

He nodded.

She sighed and looked at the cottage. "Then let's get to it."

11

The door burst open. "What in the blazes is going on here?" Hamish demanded.

Ro's head jerked up. Unfortunately, Clement was leaning over her, and her head crashed into his. "Ow!"

Clement grabbed his nose and sat down, hard.

"Oh, Clement, I am so sorry! Are you all right?"

He nodded and waved her back.

She glared at the wagon master. "Look what you made me do!"

Hamish rushed around the room, gathering an armful of the gold and trinkets they'd collected from the chamber below the cottage. "Oh no, you don't. Put these things back right now!"

Ro frowned at him. "But how am I going to pay you guys or bring France's wealth back if I put them away?" She waved her hand toward the piles of gold. "This belongs to my people, not me."

Hamish's eyes widened. "Are you crazy? I ain't touching cursed gold." He glanced down at his armful and flung it away. It clacked and bounced across the floor.

Ro moaned. "We just separated that."

Hamish pointed at Clement. "You, outside with your vegetables." Clement ran out the door, hand still over his nose. Hamish pointed at Ro next. "You. We need to talk."

He spun and stalked out the door. Ro followed, not knowing what else to do. Might as well get it over with.

Hamish spun to face her the moment they reached the back of the house. He shoved a calloused finger in her face. "You need to stop."

Ro crossed her arms. There were few things she hated more than bossy people. "Stop what?"

"Giving him hope."

She leaned forward, glare firmly in place. "I'd like to give both of you hope, only you won't let me."

He scratched his scraggly beard and paced before her, back and forth, back and forth. "Listen, let's say you're telling the truth."

"I am."

"And you really do want to free us and break this curse."

"I do."

He whirled on her and shouted in her face. "Then you don't touch blood money!"

"I—uh—what?"

He waved his arms around. "Blood money! The gold. Don't touch it. Leave it alone."

Ro rubbed her hands down her face. "I'm sorry. I'm completely at a loss."

Hamish went back to his pacing. "How do you think the witches acquired so much gold? Where do you think it came from?"

Ro raised an eyebrow. "Um, from the vegetables. What else?"

He shook his head furiously. Ro missed the laid-back guy from before. "No. Well, yes, but no. Blood money. Before France needed food, her people needed curses broken, curses placed, and all manner of unseemly things done by the rich and the greedy."

Ro crossed her arms. She didn't have time for this. "Get to the point."

"Before they got in the business of farming, a very convenient profession, I might add, the Mesdemoiselles of the Mountain were involved in many appalling practices. That gold is blood money, pure and simple."

Ro leaned forward, temper barely under control. "Let me make one thing very clear, Hamish—may I call you Hamish? Good. I don't care where the money came from; it belongs to the people of France. I don't care where the food came from; it belongs to the people of France. And I will do all within my power to make sure it gets back to where it belongs. Your only concern is to teach me to hunt so I can provide for myself. Are we clear?"

Hamish stared at her, jaw ticking. "Oui, Mademoiselle."

Ro nodded toward the wagon. "Keep filling it. My people are starving."

He nodded and moved toward the wagon without another word.

"Oh, and Hamish?"

He glanced back at her.

"Do not call me Mademoiselle here. My name is Ro."

He gave a curt nod and stomped away.

Ro turned back to her new house. It was purging time.

A bonfire lit the clear night sky. Orange danced off the full leaves, and Ro drank in the sight. If only Cosette could see all the beauty here!

The burn pile had been cleared of furniture—to be returned to the original owners, if possible—and now was full to bursting with books, scrolls, and dead animal parts.

Clement managed a whisper next to her. He'd been jumpy since she'd touched the first volume of witchcraft. "Aren't you scared?"

Ro snorted. "No, why would I be?"

Clement nodded at the blazing flames. "Them spell books carry mighty curses. Ain't you scared one of them might come back on you fer burning them?"

Ro squared her jaw. She didn't expect him to understand; she just knew what needed to be done. "Not in the least."

"Well"—he glanced to his either side—"don't you want to know how to break the curses?" At Ro's blank look, he continued. "Them books probably say how."

Ro leaned toward him and dropped her voice. "Do you really want me to become the next Mademoiselle of the Mountain?"

His eyes widened, and he shook his head.

"Then it's best I not read any spells, oui?"

"Oui."

Ro shook her head with a smirk and poked one of the books deeper into the flame. As well as she knew her own name, she knew the moment she walked into the house that the place needed to be rid of filth. All of it.

And that included every spell book and dead animal part in the house. The herbs had other uses besides witchcraft, but everything else needed to go. And Hamish and Clement had watched her in wide-eyed wonder the entire time.

She glanced at her now-silent companions. "You can both go to bed."

"What about you?"

She nodded at the pile. "I'm not going to bed until only ash remains."

Clement folded his arms. "Then neither am I."

Hamish hunkered down on the other side of the fire and poked at another book.

Ro grinned. She just might win them over yet.

12

Ro jerked awake, a long stick jabbing her side. She grabbed the stick out of reflex and tugged. Hamish almost toppled over her. She rolled out of the way. "What are you doing?" she hissed, crouched and ready to defend herself.

She glanced at a snoring Clement, his feet propped in front of the glowing embers, jacket clamped tightly around him.

"Teaching you to hunt, if you're up for it."

Ro raised her eyebrows. "Before it's even light?"

Hamish nodded. "Best time for it. Grab your crossbow and your bolts. Got anything else to wear?"

Ro glanced down at herself and shook her head.

"Then bring a blanket. It'll be cold."

Ro struggled to her feet, blinking the sleep away from her eyes. Energy surged through her. At last! She could be all Cosette needed and more.

She hurried into the cottage, downed a glass of water, freshly drawn from the well, then used the outhouse behind the cottage. She left the blanket where it lay. Pascal's jacket, worn though it was, would have to do.

In no time, she rushed to the wagon to retrieve her weapons and wait for Hamish. He approached and took the crossbow from her, settling it into a holster on his back. Without a word, he headed into the brush, away from the path that had led them to this place.

Ro followed. After a while, a thought occurred to her. "Hey! How are you able to leave?"

He shushed her, then said in a low voice, "Because I am fulfilling my promise to you."

Ro growled. His being unable to leave or not had nothing to do with her.

He shushed her again. "First rule of hunting, complete silence. Your prey shouldn't even hear your footsteps."

Ro immediately focused on every step she took and on the noises surrounding her. As she focused, the sound of her footsteps faded away. She somehow missed every twig and leaf underfoot. She could still hear Hamish's footsteps, however.

Hamish whirled around, frown firmly in place. "You still there?"

"Of course. Can't you see me?"

Hamish squinted, and Ro cocked her head. Hamish blinked. "Oh, well, stay close."

Hamish was very, very strange. And Ro had met her fill of strange people.

"Second rule: Be aware of your surroundings. Every flutter of a bird's wings. Every rustle of a blade of grass in the wind. Know where your prey is before it knows you're there. Stay alert." Hamish stopped. "Listen."

Ro stopped. Listened. A flitter of something there. A flutter of something nearby. Heavy tread of a noiseless beast. Ro blinked. A leaf turning just so and brushing another.

Ro grasped blindly for Hamish's arm and found it. "There's something there."

Hamish took several deep breaths and dislodged her hand. "Oui, I smell it. Let's get high."

After a few more steps, Hamish began climbing a tree. Ro followed him, her hands grasping each place his had, and she scaled the tree with ease. Hamish turned once he'd made it to a level perch and reached out his hand. He jumped when he saw how close she was to him.

She offered an apologetic smile—unsure if he could even see it—and turned to peer into the dark woods.

She listened to every noise surrounding her, every breath of wind caressing her face, and noticed something else.

"The air here—it is sweet. And it's not cold." She looked at Hamish. She could easily see him, though the moon didn't shine. "We're still on the witch's property, aren't we?"

"Yes, now be quiet."

"But what was that about—?"

"Shh!"

She settled back and listened, assessing and dismissing each sound as it came to her. There. The near-silent pad of heavy paws. She zoned in on the sound, and her vision soon followed. Her eyes widened, and she grabbed Hamish's arm. "A panther! Here? But how?"

He shook off her grasp. "Unhand me, girl! Yes, of course it's a panther, but"—he squinted at her—"how in the blazes do you know that?"

She pointed at the approaching creature. "It's right there. Fifty paces, coming this way. Black coat, gold eyes." She clutched at his sleeves. "Is it going to eat us?" she rasped in a hoarse whisper.

"Touch me again, and I will throw you from this tree, curse or no curse."

Ro snatched her hand back.

"Now, to answer your question, no, it's not going to eat us. Though how you can see the creature at this distance is beyond me. And how do I know it's not going to eat us?" Hamish took Père's crossbow from his back and handed it to her. "Because you're going to shoot it."

Ro's eyes widened, and she stared between the crossbow

and the man's face. The crazy, insane man, who could trade places this instant with Madame Savon.

"Me?" she squeaked. "I've never shot anything in my life! I only killed the wolf by accident, and with a knife, I might add. My family traps their food…"

"And you killed a witch with a bolt of lightning."

Ro nodded. "Which was an accident, too, by the way." She tried to shove the crossbow back at him.

He kept it firmly in her grasp. "And now you will shoot the panther. Not on accident."

Ro aimed the crossbow at the approaching creature. "Where did it even come from? Are panthers invading France now along with the wolves?"

"Load it. That's right. Cock it back. No, use your boot, girl. Pull it back with all your might till it clicks. There you go. Now aim."

Ro's trembling hands grasped the heavy weapon.

Hamish sighed. "Looks like we're going to have to work on building your strength, too."

Ro shot him a glare.

He must've felt, rather than seen, her gesture. He raised one hand, the other supporting the weapon. "Easy to do with good rest, proper nutrition, and hard work."

Ro sought out the creature. It gazed at her, just as she gazed at him.

Then it happened.

The creature's every feature lit up, blazing as if the sun shone on it full-force, casting a glow on the things around it. Slightly different than last time, but still unnatural.

Ro sucked in a breath. "Do you see that?"

"See what? I see nothing in this dark. I only know what I smell. What I hear. You're terrible at being quiet, you know."

"So are you," she shot back.

He shrugged. "So he hunts us as we hunt him. You see him?"

"I do." Her words came out breathless, full of awe.

She felt Hamish's unsettling gaze on her. "Now pull back the trigger, slowly, gently." She did. "Fix your eye on the target. Keep squeezing."

"You never told me where it came from."

"No talking. Deep breath. Now."

Ro released the bolt. It flew forward, swift, silent, deadly. It struck the beast, and a sound like a woman's scream pierced the air.

Ro's heart nearly leapt from her chest. "What was that?" she cried.

"Again! Again!" Something heavy crashed through the woods.

Ro fumbled with a bolt, clumsily sliding it into place. She'd just wedged her boot in the strap when the creature reached their tree. She gasped and yanked back. The bolt fell from its perch in the crossbow to the ground below. The panther jumped up the tree, claws outstretched, then fell to the ground, dead, its unearthly glow snuffed out in an instant.

Ro stared between the beast and Hamish. "Did you do that?"

Hamish shook his head, trembling, knife in hand. "No, you must have struck its heart. A near-perfect mark." His voice held awe, tinged with suspicion. "In the dark."

She stared at the ground, still marveling how the panther's light had snuffed out with its life force. She glared at Hamish. "What is a panther doing here, and not in wild jungles elsewhere?"

He shrugged and began his descent. "The witches kept all manner of beasts for their entertainment.

Ro felt sick. And she'd just killed a beautiful creature for hers.

As if sensing her thoughts, Hamish stopped and glared at her. "Creatures that, if they escape this cage they've been placed in, will tear your people to shreds."

Ro cocked her head. That was one way of looking at it.

Hamish dropped to the ground below. "Now help me with this thing. If you're going to kill something, then you're going to clean it and dispose of what you don't use, too."

Ro scrambled down beside him. They worked silently, Hamish showing her how to gut it and skin it by the light of an ever-so-slightly lightening sky. She worked hard, though her arms grew heavy and weak from the rush of adrenaline leaving her.

A slight noise caught her attention, and she glanced up. A panther, a second panther, smaller, lighter in color, yet no less deadly, flew through the air, right at Hamish. A line of crimson slashed across its neck, and blood sprayed, before the thing toppled Hamish, raking him wide open. Hamish lay on the ground, mouth opening and closing, horror drenching his eyes as his blood drenched the ground.

The panther's mouth clamped over his face.

Ro gasped, and the creature was back in the air, flying toward them again, Hamish completely oblivious. Without a thought, Ro grabbed his knife and lunged at the creature, slashing its throat wide open. Only this time, she wrapped her arms around it and fell sideways, away from Hamish.

They landed with a hard *thwack*, and the panther writhed for just a moment before lying still. Ro extracted herself from the panther's embrace and sat next to it, staring, shaking, and closer to sobbing than she cared to admit.

"Look at me."

Ro's head jerked up, and she stared into Hamish's concerned face. His perfectly fine, not-bleeding face.

She'd done it again. She'd seen something before it happened and had been able to stop it.

Hamish snuffed out his concerned look. She wasn't certain how many times he'd said it, but she realized she'd heard it several times before she understood what he was saying.

"Are you well, Mademoi—Ro?"

She nodded, teeth chattering.

He raised an eyebrow. "So you need me to teach you how to hunt, do you?"

"This is my first time. I swear it."

"Uh-huh." He picked up his knife and eyed the smaller panther. "I'd forgotten about the female. I'm glad you were with me."

Ro didn't bother pointing out that he wouldn't be out here —in danger—if not for her.

"Well, let's clean this one too and get them back."

"We aren't going to eat them, are we?" Ro wrinkled her nose. She wasn't sure she could eat anything after what she'd just seen.

He just looked at her.

"Can't you take them to someone who needs them more than we do?"

He eyed her thoughtfully. "If that's what you want."

Ro rubbed her belly, the memory of being stuffed full the night before with all the food she could have hoped for and more warming her. It had been so long since she'd experienced such a glorious thing. "It is."

He stood. "We still need to take them back with us."

Ro groaned and struggled to her feet. Longest night of her life.

13

"You know, I've been thinking."

"Mm?" Ro didn't pay Clement much mind. He was a chatterbox once he'd decided Ro wasn't going to tear his heart out in his sleep. Ro shuddered. He had a gruesome mind, that one. Of course, that was to be expected, living with whom he had. She dug back into her butternut squash, tender and juicy from the fire, dripping with real, actual butter. Heaven itself didn't have better food than this. It couldn't. It wasn't possible better food existed.

"My cousin said a ghost's terrorizing their town. Ever since the curse and all. Well, I was thinking—think you can kill it too?"

Ro's heart sank, and she nearly choked. Hunting animals was one thing, but a ghost? Killing the witch had been an accident. Thank the Creator she only had to face the one, not three. How would she even begin to know what to do with a ghost?

"Um, I don't think it works that way…"

Clement continued, undeterred. "And goblins are eatin' what's left of the livestock in Vinsborough, though the huntsmen are trying to convince everyone it's just wolves.

Yet not one of them—the huntsmen or the wolves—will set foot near the town. Think you can rid them of the creatures?"

Ro glared at Clement. "Are you kidding me?"

"Ah." Apparently Hamish had decided to join the fun. "You banished the witch to the netherworld faster'n Clement here can skin a rabbit. I say you should go."

Ro turned the brunt of her scowl on Hamish. "Do you even hear yourself? Ghosts? Goblins? What's next, ghouls?"

He pointed at her, his meat speared on the tip of his knife. She shuddered. That knife had been places. She would never want to eat off it.

"You have a gift, young lady, and you want to use it for good. So do this." He muttered under his breath. "Though I ain't convinced you ain't a witch yerself."

"I heard that, Hamish. I'm sitting right here."

"The point is, you need to make a name for yourself. I've taught you all I know, and I barely even taught you that. The things you know and the things you can do are uncanny. It ain't natural."

Ro tore into her butternut squash, all desire for eating meat squelched by the many things she'd killed. "So you've been telling. For months."

He waved that knife around as if it were a flag. "You want to make a difference? You want to help?"

"What do you think I've been doing?"

"You want to get off your sorry behind and stop hiding in this little haven?"

Clement snickered.

She pointed her spoon at him, far less threatening than the knife. "Hey now. Nothing from you. You started all this, you know. And is that what you call all the work I've been doing around here? Sitting on my behind?"

He laughed and kept eating, thoroughly enjoying himself. At her expense.

Ro sighed. At least they were both comfortable with her now.

Hamish took to tearing into his meat, mouth full and wide open for all to see. Ro set her butternut squash to the side and waited for him to finish.

"The world is marching on out there, Ro. And it's leaving you behind."

Ro decided she was hungry and didn't really care about Hamish's fireside manner. She had brothers, after all. She picked up her squash and dug in. Cinnamon apples would be next. Yum and yum.

"Gautier is picking up the pieces you've given the people of France, claiming them as his own doing."

Ro shrugged. She really didn't care. It was ideal. She was slowly helping her people rebuild their lives, providing food, valuables, and funds in exchange for hard work, and she didn't have to have anything to do with them. It was paradise.

Hamish had brought back news of her family's wellbeing after his many trips, and that was good enough for Ro. Who cared if someone else got the credit?

"Gautier—I've heard of him. Who is he again?"

Both Hamish and Clement stopped eating, staring at her with wide eyes. "Only the most powerful man in France!" burst from Clement's mouth.

"Oh?" She licked a golden stream of butter trying to escape down the husk of her squash.

Hamish glared at her. "You never pay attention to my stories, do you?"

Ro swallowed, a rush of heat creeping up her neck. "Of course I do." It wasn't that she didn't pay attention; she only paid attention to the important parts. The parts about people eating, about them earning livres again—the parts about her family.

"Yes, the most important man in France. A man you should know."

Ro pointed her spoon at him, brandishing the thing like a weapon. "If you are thinking marriage, you can forget it. I'm not marrying anyone."

Hamish rolled his eyes, and Clement turned beet red.

"Saints preserve us. Of course I'm not suggesting matrimony. I'm suggesting you work for him. Make a name for yourself."

Ro shrugged, going back to her meal.

"I think he would be ecstatic to meet the huntress who vanquished the Mesdemoiselles of the Mountain and has been having her lackey bring him such magnificent game as she's been hunting."

Ro's head jerked up. "What?"

Hamish grinned, smug, proud of himself. The devil.

"You didn't."

"I did, and I'm not sorry."

The flame in the fire pit gusted higher. "You will be."

He stared between the blaze and her. Now it was his turn to swallow. "Oh?"

She rolled her eyes. "That wasn't me, halfwit."

"Then explain it."

She growled, low in her throat. "It was just a breeze."

"It wasn't, and you know it."

Ro shook her head, refusing to believe it. "I killed a wolf. By accident. I killed a witch. By accident."

"You killed those panthers—"

Her head whipped up. "Both by accident!"

"How?"

"Lucky shot and lucky guess."

"And all the game you've hunted since then?"

Ro opened her mouth, but nothing came out.

"The many other creatures you've killed? Perfectly?"

Ro whispered this time. "Accident. Had to be."

"Mon Dieu, I've never seen anyone hunt as you do. You have a gift, child."

"Then I'll use it. Here." She jabbed at her meal.

Hamish shook his head and looked to Clement for backup. Clement jumped and shook his head too. Hamish nodded, satisfied.

"Non. Wolves still prey on your people, as you won't stop calling them. The curse may not allow them to die of starvation, but it certainly doesn't repel wolf attacks."

Ro refused to answer.

"Ro. Look at me."

Ro lifted her eyes to meet Hamish's. She hated herself for it, but her eyes filled with tears.

"It is time for you to leave this place. To do what you were called to do. To break this curse."

"I am breaking it."

"No, you are lessening its effects. Little by little. But the curse remains."

Ro's eyes drifted to the lush garden. "And if I leave this place? You said it was open to me, but the last time I left, I could barely find the place. What if I can never find it again?"

Hamish shrugged. "You might not be able to. I don't know. But we will be right here, doing our tasks, until they are no longer necessary, or until it is the right time for you to find us again."

Ro stared at the fire, tears dripping from her chin. "That's not fair to you. And how do you even know this?"

"How did you know to kill that panther?"

Ro didn't answer.

"In the same way, I know it is time for you to leave this place, and I know we will be fine."

Ro stared into the fire for a long time—they all did—until Ro tossed in the rest of her dinner and rolled herself in her blanket, settling before the fire. Dessert forgotten.

Ro woke the next morning to hazy light, no fire, and a blackened landscape. She bolted upright, panic clawing at her throat.

The garden was gone, the cottage was gone, and all the greenery that she had loved so much—gone.

Ro cried out and untangled herself from her bedroll, running to where the garden had once been.

The stench of decay hit her nose with every footfall. She'd forgotten how much the curse made the land stink.

She stood in the middle of the nonexistent garden, mouth hanging open. Had it been another dream? Had she fallen asleep in the wagon? Had the wagon master dumped her here the first chance he got?

It was too much. She covered her face with her hands and sobbed. Oh, how she ached for the last months to be true! She'd been somebody important. She'd mattered.

She'd made a difference.

"Why are you crying?"

Ro choked back her tears and swiped her face, searching for the voice. "I'm not." She cleared her throat and tried to find her best glare.

"And do you make a habit of lying, Mademoiselle Rosette Jacqueline Reynard?"

Ro choked for real this time. "Who are you?"

A shimmering creature came into view—the most beautiful woman Ro had seen in her life—tall, lithe, graceful. Ro bowed on one knee. "Forgive me, Madame. I did not see you."

Knowing she should bow was as natural as breathing, though Ro couldn't have explained the knowledge to anyone who asked.

"Your manservant is right. It is time you leave this place and fight for your people."

Ro snorted. She'd like the fairy to call Hamish a manservant to his face. Wait, she was talking to a fairy? Not just any fairy—the Queen of the Fairies. Now, how in the blazes did she know that? And where were her wings? Didn't fairies have wings?

"Not unless we need them, and oui, I am the Queen of the Fairies, and my charge is waiting to meet you. Quite desperately, I might add."

"Uh…" That was Ro. Miss Eloquent. Where was Cosette when she needed her?

"You will see your sister in time. Now, will you do as I ask? Will you leave this place and seek your fate?"

All Ro wanted to say was, "No, I am quite happy here, thank you very much," but instead she found herself saying, "Yes, Madame. Right away."

Pleasure filled the beautiful, sparkling creature, a hidden light glimmering within, very much like her white rose. "Good. I will tell him to expect you and not to despair."

Ro frowned. Him? Did she mean Gautier? And what of the garden?

"It is hidden from your sight. For now." The queen held out her hand. "The flower, if you please."

Ro's hand trembled as she slipped the white rose from her pocket and held it out to the woman. The fairy gently lifted it from her fingers, and it melted into her hand like snow on a warm day.

"I accept your gift and offer my own in return." She leaned forward and kissed Ro's forehead. Warmth flooded her, joy as she'd never felt, happiness, love, peace. Ro scrambled to her feet and jumped back, and the feelings faded.

"What—what do I—what was that?" No, that wasn't right. "What do you want me to do?" Yes, that is what she wanted to ask. But still… "What did you do?" Ro clamped her mouth shut. Enough babbling, already!

"Go. It will all become clear to you. The Creator be with you."

Ro bowed her head. "And with you, Madame."

The tall woman vanished, and once again Ro was assaulted by the stench of the land.

Well, this was just great. She'd made a promise to a powerful queen, and she had no idea what she'd just promised. Typical.

She shouldered her pack, checked her many weapons, and slipped her crossbow in the holster on her back. She glanced down at her lean, tanned, and muscular arms, then breathed out a sigh of relief. Oh, good. It hadn't been a dream.

She glanced around her. "I'll be back, Hamish. Clement. Take care of the place for me. And go home if you can."

She headed straight for Gautier's château, the distance melting away in a glance, her path made clear to her. A gift from the queen? Perhaps.

She grinned. Wouldn't they be shocked to meet a person who'd been kissed by sunlight?

14

So Gautier had refused to see her. So what? It just meant Ro had to work that much harder to convince him that she was who she said she was—that her reputation was truly her own.

Not that she cared. Well…apparently she did. Hence why she was dragging her latest kill before him.

Ro hefted the wolf pelt from her shoulders. It landed before the throne with a soft rush of sound and the clack of nails.

The man sitting there eyed it, then raised his eyes to meet hers. "You expect me to believe you killed this poor creature yourself? No help."

Ro lifted her chin. "Yes, sir."

Everyone in the court laughed, including this Gautier she'd heard so much about. The man's père had once been the king's steward, a man who'd tried and failed miserably to hold the kingdom together after the curse had taken effect. Now Gautier had convinced the people he could rule in the king's— and his père's—stead. Ro found it intriguing the man even remembered they had a king and daunting that still no one else remembered or cared about their missing rulers. Now this upstart was promising food, a future, and freedom from the curse. Promises Ro very much wondered if he could keep.

Interest lit his eyes. She kept the light from her own. She had him.

He eyed the pelt. "And where is the meat?"

"I sold it in the village, then cured the coat, just as your instructions stated."

"By yourself."

His smile made her want to sprint across the room and scratch out his eyes. She took a deep, calming breath, determined to outwit her prey.

She refused to break eye contact. "By myself."

The rest of the court continued their heckling, but Gautier kept one fist over his still-smiling mouth, eyes considering. He lowered his hand. "Bring me another. Treasurer, pay her."

The laughter silenced, the treasurer spluttered, but soon she had a heavy pouch in her hands.

She nodded and slipped the coin purse within her leather jacket. "As you wish."

She turned and left, holding back her smile until she was outside of the small château.

Soon her sister would have everything she wished for and more. And she could return to her home in the mountains, never to be bothered again.

Ro stomped away from yet another village.

It didn't matter how many times things had gone right, she still couldn't figure out *how* she did it.

This time, she'd simply walked into the village, and the spirit terrorizing the people had left, shrieking the whole way, its trail of wispy, white smoke dissipating into nothing.

The people had cheered, thrown her a feast, paid her handsomely, and sent her on her way, scared out of their minds of her, no matter how much they praised her and smiled at her.

Ro didn't blame them. She had no idea how she worked either. She'd never again been able to conjure a storm, make a fire blaze, or see something before it happened as she had before. Every time, something different happened. It was driving her crazy.

At least her prey still lit up the night like daylight, but only when she was hunting.

She fingered the heavy pouch, clinking with gold coins.

Now that she received the same payment the Mesdemoiselles of the Mountain once received—though she tried to come up with creative ways to give it back to the townspeople—was hired by villagers all over France, and was paid handsomely by Gautier himself, she should soon have more than enough for Cosette. But desperation spurred her on.

Would she earn it in time? Would her père accept that he no longer owed the castle's beast any one of his daughter's lives?

And how long until Père decided to send Cosette in Ro's stead? She was the youngest, after all.

An inkling of an idea had begun the last time she'd scoped out her family's refurbished home, and it had grown into a full-fledged mission.

Cosette needed to be far from her family, too. Far away from the curse. Far away from her lunatic père.

Somewhere she was safe, somewhere she could be the lady she was, somewhere…also far from Ro and her soiled reputation, in case anyone discovered who her family was.

She almost had enough.

Just a few more jobs from Gautier, and she could do it. She shook her head. Had she known she needed so much to pay the priest and Madame LaChance for Cosette's safe passage, she would've never returned all the witches' gold to the people.

Though they needed it, Cosette needed it more. And Madame LaChance would not be bargained down in price.

Way to think it through, Ro, way to think it through…

She grabbed her horse's bridle and untied him from a tree. She led him to a stump and scrambled up on it, mounting the horse that was easily twenty hands high. Most people shied away from the massive beast, but Ro didn't mind.

That meant it kept people away from her too.

She nudged him from the village, wishing the entire time she could solve the mystery that was herself. And keep Cosette safe, once and for all.

Ro kept her head down as she hurried through the village, hoping her cloak's hood and the horse at her side would keep her fairly anonymous.

They didn't. She should've known better, especially with her giant of a horse and her vibrant-red cloak. Was any other hunter as conspicuous as she? Whispers followed her down the street.

"The huntress!"

"It's the huntress!"

"What is she doing here?"

"On a personal mission for Monsieur Gautier, no doubt."

"I wonder what she looks like? It's rumored no one has seen her face, not even Gautier himself."

Ro snorted at that one. She had a feeling the townsfolk would be highly disappointed to discover the mighty huntress was once their feisty little nobody.

Her horse stumbled to a halt, and she right alongside him.

"Fairweather, what—? Oh."

Madame Savon stood before them, blocking their path, and pointed one long, crooked finger at Ro. "Keep to this path, and it will claim you. You will *die*!"

Ro jerked back and hurried away, subconsciously and perhaps a little superstitiously taking another way to her family's home. Crazy old bat. Ro didn't come home often, but she needed to see her sister. She didn't know why; she just had to.

Her run-in with Madame Savon was unfortunate. She didn't want to be connected with her family. It was why she adopted a new surname.

She had to protect them at all costs. Especially her sister.

She gave her family's home a wide berth and headed straight for her treehouse. Her family was back in their country house. They couldn't yet afford to live in the city, but Ro had made them comfortable enough to ensure they could move into the opulent dwelling. She sat in her treehouse, lit the lamp, and waited, watching the bustle of country life below.

Ah, they had a new serving maid. That made a cook, a butler, a footman, a stableman, and three maids. She watched them scurry about their daily tasks. They seemed to be working hard. Perhaps the family was in?

Cosette came in and out of view, and Ro's heart leapt. She leaned forward, peering through the wooden railing as Cosette flitted in and out of view of the different windows. Ro had no hope Cosette would see the light until dusk had fallen, but how she ached to speak with her now. This very minute. To be welcomed into her old home with open arms and be treated like a sister again.

A wry grin touched her mouth. Yes, even if that meant being picked on by her five pests. Cosette excluded, of course.

Her brothers weren't home. She'd already peeked into their places of apprenticeship. Pascal was studying to become a banker, and Claude, a silver worker. It'd only taken a small nudge to connect them with what they both enjoyed doing. Their employers loved having such hard and competent workers, and her brothers loved being away from their sisters.

And they would never know Ro had seen to it that they

came highly recommended to the shop owners. And she'd never tell. Now a full-fledged grin touched her lips.

Her brothers. Hard workers. Who knew?

Now Cosette climbed the winding stairs to the upper floor. Ro held her breath and pressed her face against the slats. Could she possibly see her sister soon, not hours from now? But no, it would be hard to see the lit lamp in the daylight, but Ro's heart refused to listen to her. She so badly wanted to curl up with her sister and trade secrets and be normal again.

But her life would never be normal. Not since she'd chosen to be a huntress, and not since she'd overheard her sisters say their bad luck was her fault—because of the rose—and their misfortunes had only reversed once she'd left.

Their misfortune had befallen them long before she'd received the rose, but her sisters didn't care.

And they were partly right. They'd had Père back—until he'd given her the rose.

She shook the melancholy thoughts from her when Cosette turned her way on the staircase, glanced toward the treehouse, and froze. Her face lit with joy, and she ran down the staircase.

Ro laughed and bounced. It was too good to be true!

Several excruciating minutes later, Cosette was scrambling up the ladder to the old tree fort, and Ro blew out the lantern.

Cosette tackled her in a hug. "Oh, my dearest Rosette!"

Ro laughed and hugged her back fiercely. "Hush, you! You don't want anyone to overhear." She tugged up the rope ladder.

Cosette hushed her voice but set about squealing and bouncing in the most unladylike manner. "I wasn't expecting another visit so soon! What brings you? Not that I mind. Not in the least. Oh, I'm so happy to see you!"

Ro's smile stayed plastered on her face, but she didn't know how to answer that. "I can't say. I really can't. I've got another job"—Cosette's expression dimmed, but only for a moment, and she desperately tried to cover it—"and I had to see you. How are things?"

Ro's smile felt wooden. Knowing her sister disapproved, even the slightest, hurt more than it should've. Everyone else in the world could disapprove if only her sister were on her side.

Ro slammed the trap door closed a little harder than she meant to, and Cosette jumped. Ro offered an apologetic smile as Cosette launched into a monologue of every word and action of their five sisters and two brothers. Neither mentioned Père, as it had been since he'd flown into a rage the first time she'd visited, denouncing her and not allowing her entrance. She'd never even been inside the updated version of her old house.

"So they like their apprenticeships?"

"Like them?" Cosette laughed. "You should see them strutting about. A banker. And a precious-metal worker." She lifted her nose in the air and struck a snooty pose. Both girls dissolved into giggles.

It felt so good to laugh.

Cosette shook her head. "I think they're proud to be good at something. To work with their hands and take care of their family." A sly look entered her eyes. "Something tells me they didn't quite get us this house on their own, however."

Ro shrugged and winked. "And whatever would I possibly know about that?"

Cosette smiled, looking no less satisfied than a cat with a bowl full of cream. "I thought so." Her eyes drifted over Ro's red cloak. "I see you still wear Mère's cloak. It fits you well."

Ro reached for the strings. "You're welcome to—"

Cosette stopped her, covering Ro's hand with her own. "Don't you dare. It was a gift. Really. I want you to have it."

Ro smiled, and Cosette chuckled and began a story about Reinette's latest mishap. The awkward girl loved to throw herself at any eligible bachelor and could never tell when the young man had a glaring lack of interest, lending many a tale to Cosette, and far too many giggles to Ro.

Finally, the sisters grew quiet, and worry flitted across Cosette's face.

Ro tensed. "What? What is it?"

"Nothing, I—"

"Cosette. You must tell me. The smallest thing could be of great import. I keep my association quiet with all of you for a reason."

Cosette took a deep breath. "You're not going to like it."

Ro's jaw hardened. "There isn't much I like in this world. Spit it out."

Cosette fiddled with her dress, creasing the fine fabric. "Père is…seeing someone."

Ro instantly felt lightheaded as all the blood drained from her face.

Cosette held her breath, watching Ro carefully. Ro tried to minimize her reaction for Cosette's sake, but she just couldn't manage it. Ro felt as if someone had delivered a right hook and left her reeling.

"Seeing…someone." She couldn't wrap her mind around it.

The details poured out of her sister's mouth. "She is a countess. Very wealthy from what I've heard. Oh, nothing grows in her gardens—she still has to rely on food from the new Mademoiselle of the Mountain, just like everyone else—"

Ro smirked. Yeah, Cosette—and the rest of the country— had no clue about all the details surrounding the three witches. Or her. And she'd keep it that way if she could.

"But she didn't barter everything away, so she still has some standing in her community."

"Does Père…like…her?"

Cosette shrugged, not meeting her eyes. "He doesn't *not* like her."

"What on earth does that mean?"

Cosette looked at her then, misery etched in every feature.

"I think he's thinking of her fortune, his daughters, and her daughters. Maybe a grasp at happiness?"

Ro could barely force the words past the burning in her throat. "Her…daughters? Has he forgotten Mère so soon?"

Cosette took both of Ro's hands into her own. "It's been almost fifteen years, dearest Rose. We mustn't begrudge him a chance at happiness."

Ro was suddenly glad she'd been kicked out. She'd never step foot in her père's home again.

"Cosette? Cosette!"

Both girls jumped. Ro would recognize that voice anywhere. Bernadette. Good *night* but the girl could screech.

"Oh, no! I forgot!" Cosette scrambled for the exit hatch and ladder.

Desperation seized Ro. She still hadn't told Cosette what she came to tell her. "Wait! Where are you going?"

Cosette lifted the door and fed the ladder into the hole. "There is a soirée at Madame Chevyon's tonight. I must get ready now if we are to attend on time." She rolled her eyes, a very un-Cosette-like gesture. "Thanks to you, we now have to re-enter polite society and deal with suitors, parties, and everything else dreadful that comes with it."

"Oh, you love all that, and you know it."

Cosette's grin was rather impish. "I do." She swung her feet over the edge.

"Wait! Please. I have something I need to tell you."

Cosette paused on the first step of the swinging rope. She clung to the edge. "Hurry. Or I fear discovery."

Ro leaned close. "I have another job—"

"Cosette! Don't make me come find you," Bernadette caterwauled.

Cosette dropped down one more step.

Ro hesitated. "I will send you a letter through one of our brothers. Obey every word, especially if Père remarries. Promise me."

"I promise." Cosette launched her petite frame at Ro, hanging on for one last desperate hug before she continued down the contrary rope.

Ro watched her go, then pulled up the rope and secured the hatch. Her heart broke into a million pieces as Cosette ran toward the house and the hollering Bernadette on the front steps. Bernadette brushed Cosette's skirts, looking as if she were scolding her with every word she flung her sister's way.

Ro groaned and propped her back against the rough wall.

She needed to talk to Cosette, but she had to set off for Gautier's tonight. He had a job for her—a rather lucrative one—and he wanted it kept a secret.

A job for her only. Not for any of his trusted huntsmen, whom she often worked with, though she preferred to work alone.

The very thought gave her chills. She should've been flattered, but something was off.

She just felt like she needed to say goodbye to Cosette, provide for Cosette, one final time.

And she had no idea why.

15

"I've found her."

Up until this point, Magic looked completely bored. She sat, twirling her hair, eyes staring off into the distance, seconds from severing their connection. Now she bolted upright, fingers clenching the throne she was sitting in. The king's throne. Left vacant for many years. Gautier caught just a glimpse of the wreckage and decay behind her.

"What? Who?"

"The girl. The huntress. She can see the castle."

"What girl?" The woman's pale face matched her washed-out surroundings. Gautier held his smirk in check. She hadn't been that pale a few seconds ago.

"She's the best huntress I have. She's smarter, faster, and more tenacious than any of my other huntsmen. And get this. She doesn't only hunt wolves." Gautier's eyes sparkled.

If anything, the woman before him tensed further. "Get on with it. Explain what you mean."

He leaned forward and dropped his voice. She matched his posture, move for move. "There are reports that she does a little hunting on the side."

The woman's eyebrows rose, and the expression on her face clearly asked why she should care.

"Reports say—now this may just be gossip—but she rids small villages of ghosts, ghouls, and goblins." He straightened and chuckled, adjusting the fur lining around his wrists. He needed to send his jacket to be combed and treated. "A few of my contacts swear that at times, she is summoned instead of the priest."

The woman sat back and laughed. "Oh, Gautier, you're worse than a woman."

His attention snapped back to her, his expression frosty.

She continued, her practiced, bored look back in place. "The only thing it takes to further gossip is to share it. You don't really believe any of that, do you?"

The outrage her words caused washed away, and the smile crept back on to Gautier's face. Nonchalant as her words sounded, an underlying ripple of tension said she cared more than she let on.

Oh, yes. He'd found the huntress he'd been looking for.

His smile beamed. "Of course not." She relaxed. "Then again—" Tension radiated from the woman. He winked. "If she truly can see the castle as she claims—and perhaps enter it?—maybe we can hire her to take care of a problem we both have, oui?"

"I see." Magic sat back, eyes hooded. "You've been planning this for quite some time, haven't you?"

Gautier smiled and bowed, neither confirming nor denying it. "Your concern is my concern."

Magic sat still, quiet, for too long. Then her eyes began to gleam, erasing some of the sparkle from Gautier's. A hint of worry wafted through him.

This woman was not to be trusted—not at all—but he thought he'd found a solution to rid him of two troublesome things at once.

One, the beast.

Two, Magic.

If the girl was as smart as she appeared. It would be so simple if only everything turned out according to plan.

"All right. Send her to me. I will ensure she enters, but it is up to you to make sure she hunts the right creature."

Gautier gave her a smug, self-satisfied smile. "I already have everything in place."

"Of course you do." Her dry comment gave him immense satisfaction. Her image slowly faded from his mirror, replacing her image with his. He turned his face side to side, admiring the strong jawline, the dark hair, the aristocratic nose.

That sister of hers—the huntress' sister—Cosette, was it? —would look lovely next to him. The only one of the bunch worth having. She would make a fine queen once the prince was out of the way and he could be crowned king of France.

And if that cursed Fairy Queen hadn't made it impossible for him to be king otherwise, he'd already be crowned and on the throne.

His scowl interrupted his enjoyment of looking at himself. He could only be king once the beast was dead, and the beast would only die if Magic let him.

Magic was toying with them both.

He smoothed out his expression and smiled. Well, he'd force her hand. She was easily manipulated with just the right word. The right gesture.

He ran his tongue over his teeth, making sure they gleamed and not a morsel remained from his lunch. Oh, yes. The girl would kill the beast, work her skill on Magic, and he would get the beautiful, innocent little sister for his bride.

It was all working out according to plan.

His conversation with Magic replayed itself in his mind. She was so sure she would win, that Gautier was her puppet. She'd been stuck in her ivory tower too long.

Haughty, cold, yet with desperation shining in her eyes... and something else...

Gautier laughed. Oh, that was priceless. The sorceress thought she held him in her control? On the contrary, he was very much the one pulling the strings.

And he'd have it no other way.

THE END

Ro's story continues in

Kill the Beast

Book One of the Beast Hunters.

Available Now from L2L2 Publishing.

ACKNOWLEDGMENTS

First of all, I praise and thank my Lord Jesus Christ for His lovely gift of storytelling. I am in awe of all the beautiful stories out there—in people's lives, in movies, online, in books, and in numerous other places—and I am humbled to be a small part of it. Wow! To think You created *me* to be a writer!

And to you, dear reader. Thank you for taking a chance on my book. Your time is precious, and I am so happy you spent some of it on me.

To my lovely beta readers: Jebraun, Laura, Kara, Tim, Sarah, Barbie, Dominique, Josh, Savannah, Alex, and Nicole. You caught so many things that just needed help, and I am eternally grateful to each one of you. And thank you for all of the encouraging comments. I'm so glad you enjoyed my story!

Lindsay A. Franklin, editor extraordinaire: You get me. You get my voice, my heart for my stories, and I adore each of your comments. (Even when I make a blazing mistake that I Just. Can't. Believe happened.) Thank you for taking time for this author! I adore you.

Sara Helwe, your covers. Your *covers*! I cherish each one you've made me, and I love working with you so much. Thank you for another gorgeous cover! I pray so many blessings for you, and for your heart's desire to come true. So much love.

And to my sweet husband, who supports me in this crazy writing adventure, and to my Blaze, Maverick, and Gwenivere, who are the best kids in the world: I love each of you so much I can hardly stand it.

If I have forgotten anyone, please know you are loved and treasured and mean the world to me.

With all my heart,
Michele

ABOUT THE AUTHOR

Michele Israel Harper spends her days as an acquisitions editor for L2L2 Publishing and her nights spinning her own tales. Sleep? Sometimes . . .

She has her Bachelor of Arts in history, is slightly obsessed with all things French—including Jeanne d'Arc and *La Belle et la Bête*—and loves curling up with a good book more than just about anything else.

Author of ten published novels (and more on the way), Michele prays her involvement in writing, editing, and publishing will touch many lives in the years to come.

Visit MicheleIsraelHarper.com or L2L2Publishing.com to keep in touch or to learn more about her!

Michele loves to hear from her readers! Follow her on social media, check out her website, or drop her a line to let her know what you thought of Beast Hunter. *Happy reading!*

www.MicheleIsraelHarper.com
Facebook: @MicheleIsraelHarper
Twitter: @MicheleIHarper
Instagram: @Michele_Israel_Harper

And sign up for her newsletter for bookish news!
MicheleIsraelHarper.com/My-Newsletter

REVIEWS

Did you enjoy the book? Please leave a review!

Did you know reviews can skyrocket a book's career? Instead of fizzling into nothing, a book will be suggested by Amazon, shared by Goodreads, or showcased by Barnes & Noble. Plus, authors treasure reviews! (And read them over and over and over . . .)

Whether you enjoyed this book or not, would you consider leaving a review on:

- Amazon
- Barnes & Noble
- Goodreads

. . . or perhaps even your personal blog or website or fave social media account? Thank you so much!

—The L2L2 Publishing Team

Ro remembers the castle before it disappeared. Now it shimmers to life one night a year, seen by her alone. Once a lady, now a huntress, Ro does what it takes to survive. A beast has overtaken the castle; a beast Ro has been hired to kill. But things are not as they seem. Trapped in the castle, a prisoner alongside the beast, Ro wonders what she should fear most: the beast, the magic that holds them both captive, or the one who hired her to kill the beast.

Silence
the
Siren
Michele Israel Harper

WHERE WILL WE TAKE YOU NEXT?

Hunt with *Kill the Beast,*
Sink into *Silence the Siren,*
Discover *Wisdom & Folly Sisters,*
Shiver with *Ghostly Vendetta,*
and Devour *Zombie Takeover.*

All at
Love2ReadLove2WritePublishing.com/Bookstore
or your local or online retailer.

Happy Reading!
~The L2L2 Publishing Team

ABOUT L2L2 PUBLISHING

Love2ReadLove2Write Publishing, LLC is a small traditional press, dedicated to clean or Christian speculative fiction.

Speculative fiction includes any fantastical element, and usually falls in the genres or subgenres of Fantasy or Science Fiction.

We seek stunning tales masterfully told, and we strive to create an exquisite publishing experience for our authors and to produce quality fiction for our readers.

Beast Hunter is at the heart of what we publish: a fairy tale that turns tropes on their heads that we hope will delight our readers.

All of our titles can be found or requested at your favorite online book retailer, local bookstore, or favorite local library.

Visit L2L2Publishing.com to view our submissions guidelines, find our other titles, or learn more about us.

And if you love our books, please leave a review!

Happy Reading!

~The L2L2 Publishing Team